New Horizons

A Mount Desert Island Series

Katie Winters

New Horizon in Bar Harbor
Mount Desert Island Series
By
Katie Winters

Chapter One

The baby grand piano stage-left in the picturesque jazz club off the Chicago Loop had a chipped D-flat/C-sharp key. In all her years of professional jazz piano, Angela Montague had never seen anything like it. The jagged and strange black key looked as though it had been chewed to bits along the base. Her index finger toyed along the sharp edges as the rest of her jazz band set up across the rest of the stage. This was it— their highest-paying gig of the entire year.

It was New Year's Eve.

Her husband of twenty-two years, Felix Montague, was renowned as the top alto-saxophonist in the jazz-heavy Chicago area. He and Angie had begun this very jazz band twelve years before and had amassed critical success. None of them in the group was a millionaire, but none went hungry, either. It was a marvel to say that you made your living playing music. Each time the transfer came into Angie and Felix's joint bank account, Angie wanted to call her father to say, "Take that." He'd demanded that she major in something more sensible. Armed with only her love of music— and then, concurrently, her dramatic love of Felix— Angie had resisted.

And miraculously, she'd made it work.

Felix still had it at forty-seven years old. He had a strong, captivating face— a nose that curved to a point, thick eyebrows, and pointed cheekbones. Ordinarily, and also tonight, his cheeks and chin sported a thick scruff. He wore all black, as was his signature. When his blue eyes found hers across the glow of the baby grand, Angie's stomach flipped backward.

The rest of the group was made up of a drummer, Eugene, who'd been with Angie and Felix from the start, along with a bassist, Autumn, who'd joined three years previous, plus a trumpet player, Tyler, and a trombonist, Jenny. Together, they were called the Lake City Rollers, a play on the band from the sixties and seventies, the Bay City Rollers.'

Felix, their leader, counted them off just before eleven p.m. After a flick of his finger, the six-piece jazz combo burst into a traditional jazz piece— "Mack the Knife," made famous by Ella Fitzgerald. Angie's wrists whisked up and down the keys; her fingers were loose and articulate as she plinked her way through the joyous tune. Already, she sensed that the audience adored them. Probably many of them had seen the Lake City Rollers in the past. People who liked jazz tended to seek out the same groups and lurk in jazz clubs such as this one. People often liked to hear variations of the same thing over and over again, if only to unwind and feel safe.

Angie didn't mind that. She could understand it, even. She'd loved Felix Montague for twenty-three years and counting. Together, they'd shared the same rent-controlled apartment in Hyde Park since their marriage. They'd even raised their daughter, twenty-year-old Hannah, there.

It had been Angie's dream to bring Hannah into the jazz ensemble after her graduation from music school. She'd been the most promising trumpet player in her graduating class and had excelled beyond all freshman and sophomores at the University of Chicago. Her abrupt departure from the university the previous autumn had cast a rift between Angie, Felix, and Hannah.

It wasn't something Angie liked to think about often. It was just difficult, especially now, mere days after Christmas and the night before the New Year. Most other New Year's Eve celebrations, Hannah had been stationed at the table nearest to Angie as she'd played in the ensemble. She liked to say that she wanted to have the best view of her mother's fingers. "You have the most intricate parts," Hannah had said. "I want to make sure I catch them."

Angie allowed the music to fold over her, flow through her. As they played through "Stella by Starlight" and "Honeysuckle Rose," she frequently forgot herself, closing her eyes to the swell of the music. When Felix announced that they would now have a countdown to midnight in the microphone, Angie nearly leaped with surprise. *Had an hour passed by already?*

"Ladies and gentleman, it's nearly that time again." Felix's voice was almost like a crooner's. He brought his arm out to the right of him, extending it toward the rest of the ensemble. The drummer placed the brush-drumsticks on the snare drum and shook them expectantly as Felix counted down. "Ten. Nine. Eight." The rest of the crowd joined along with him. Angie's heart shuddered in her ribcage.

Were they ready for another year? Could they do it? Even if Hannah never spoke to them again?

But suddenly, it was time. It was now midnight. Just as they had every other year, the Lake City Rollers burst into their version of "Auld Lang Syne" as the guests in the jazz club struggled to sing along. Over the years, people had really lost their grip on the lyrics.

They sang:

"Should auld acquaintance be forgot
And never brought to mind?
Should auld acquaintance be forgot
And days of auld lang syne?"

Angie mouthed through the words as tears welled in her eyes. When they finished the tune, she lifted her eyes expectantly toward Felix. Just like every other year, Felix jumped up from his chair and headed for her, ready for their New Year's kiss. He stopped at the edge of the piano, dropped his head low, and said, "Happy New Year, Kid," which was what he always said.

But when he leaned in to kiss her, something very strange happened.

His lips grazed across her cheek.

Her *cheek.*

Not her lips. Not his wife's lips, a wife he'd loved for twenty-three years.

For New Year's, a husband had given his wife a kiss on the cheek.

Angie shivered with the horror of it. She half-expected him to rear back, then correct himself with a kiss that rattled through her. But instead, he lifted up, turned back to the crowd, and delivered that glorious, shining grin of his. He lifted his arms on either side of him as the crowd roared joyously, most of them only just now coming up for air from their New Year's kisses, the kisses that supposedly set the mood for the next three-hundred and sixty-five days.

Her husband had given her a kiss on the cheek.

The Lake City Rollers were paid to play until one-thirty in the morning, at which time the jazz enthusiasts of the city packed themselves into cabs and got themselves home.

As the audience dispersed, their drummer, Eugene,

performed a little drumroll and then howled, "We did it, gang! Another year finished and to be logged in the books."

Felix headed for Eugene. The two men high-fived joyously. Autumn removed her bass from her shoulders and rubbed the space where the strap had been. "I need a drink," she said simply.

"I think we all do," Tyler, the trumpeter, added.

"Hey, Billy! Can we get a round of champagne up here?" Felix called down to the bartender.

Moments later, Billy uncorked the champagne bottle and poured portions into flute glasses. Angie realized she hadn't eaten anything since noon; the champagne would go straight to her head. Maybe she wanted that. When the group clanked their glasses together, Felix seemed to make eye contact with everyone in the ensemble except her, his wife.

What was going on?

"We did it again, huh?" Jenny smiled wide toward Angie, whose face probably looked shadowed and strange. "You killed it again, Angie. That solo in 'Time for a Change' blew me away."

"She played it at home until my ears bled," Felix informed Jenny.

Angie's stomach dropped lower.

"You too good for practice time these days, Felix?" Eugene teased. Nobody seemed to notice that Felix had completely soured to Angie. They assumed he was only joking. It was Felix's way.

"Who wants a cocktail?" Autumn asked excitedly as she whipped down the steps from the stage to the bar. "I'd kill for an Old Fashioned."

"Me too," Eugene called.

"Felix?" Autumn asked.

"Sure thing," Felix replied.

Angie sipped her champagne and gathered up her piano

music, most of which she no longer needed after so many years of practicing the same tracks. She placed her piano folders in her backpack and then walked down the steps, heading for the back closet. Once there, she spotted the package of cigarettes on top of Eugene's drumstick case. Angie had never been a full-time smoker, but being in the music biz meant that she'd stolen a few here and there back in the old days. Just now, as stress made her heart beat skittishly, she yearned to reach for that pack and bring one to her lips.

What was it she'd told Hannah when she had caught her out back smoking? "You have to be responsible for your health. You're the only one who has any say in how you live. And I want you to live a long time."

A headache clouded Angie's mind. She fell back against the wall and sipped the rest of her champagne flute. The sound of Jenny and Eugene celebrating curled down the hallway. This was her closest group of friends in the world. They practiced three times per week, for four hours each time, on top of two performances per week. Her social life lived and died with the jazz ensemble. She'd hardly lived a Friday or Saturday night off the stage in her entire adult life.

This meant that she had absolutely no one to speak to about her marriage— about the fact that this cheek-kiss seemed in line with several other strange factors in her recent relationship. Had it all begun when Hannah had dropped out of university and stopped taking their calls? When was the last time she and Felix had slept together? When was the last time they'd had a real conversation that had nothing to do with their musical careers? When was the last time she'd allowed herself to cry in front of him?

It was January 1st, which was meant to be a time of adventure, of new beginnings, of a fresh swell of energy. By contrast, Angie's insides felt half-dead.

"Angie!" Jenny called from down the hall. "Get back down

here! We need you."

Angie puffed out her cheeks and returned to the party. Felix and Angie had been friends with the jazz club owner since the early nineties, which meant that they were allowed to stick around all night if they wanted to. The owner himself would be there with his wife and their dearest friends. The party would probably rage till dawn, maybe as some sort of promise to themselves that they never had to grow old, not really, as long as they pretended to be youthful.

Angie sat with Jenny, Eugene, Autumn, and Tyler as Felix spoke with the jazz club owner. Autumn crossed one slender leg over the other and pinged her thumbs over her phone screen, texting someone. Autumn was a bit younger than the rest of them, mid-to-late thirties or thereabouts, and usually gave the air that she wanted to be somewhere else. Angie wanted to scream at her, "Okay! Go wherever it is you want to be!" But naturally, she held it all in.

"I have to run to the ladies' room," Autumn announced as she jumped to her feet. She then sauntered away, curving her butt this way, then that as she went.

"It was a good performance," Eugene said, slurring his words a bit.

"Yeah? You seemed to be having fun," Jenny chided. "Picking up the tempo so fast on 'So Blue.' I was like, where is his head at?"

Eugene rolled his eyes. "I did not."

"Did so."

"Felix would have said something if I had," Eugene returned.

"Felix is busy right now, but I'm pretty sure he's headed back to this table to put you in your place," Jenny said. "He's done it before."

Angie poured herself another glass of champagne and tried to drum up the courage to speak. She fell into conversation with both Jenny and Eugene about Jenny's newfound love for dating apps and her assurance that "Really, you can find great dates after forty!" Eugene scoffed and said that he'd sworn off love a long time ago. Angie tipped the rest of her champagne down her throat and then shuddered to her feet. She really should have eaten something.

Jenny and Eugene were in the midst of an argument about the fool's game of dating and hardly noticed Angie's departure. She staggered toward the hallway and paused in the shadows. She'd heard something, something strange and sinister; a part of her knew not to get closer to the source of that sound. A part of her, maybe, already knew the truth.

"You don't understand." Felix's hiss curled out through the crack in the doorway of the men's bathroom. He no longer sounded like the crooner on-stage. Rather, he sounded panicked, like an animal backed into a corner.

"What don't I understand?" The voice was Autumn's. It was unmistakable.

"We have a good thing going here," Felix continued. "The jazz ensemble has made more money in the past twelve months than ever before. We can't just..."

"Come on, Felix. We both know this is your ensemble, not hers. There are other pianists out there."

"That's bad press, Autumn, and you know it."

"Bad press? That a couple in the music business got divorced? Grow up, Felix. That story happens all the time. You know what you want. It's right in front of you. Grow a pair and leave her. Let's do what we always said we would. I love you. You know that I love you. Why would you give up on us? Why would you—"

But Autumn couldn't say all there was to be said. Instead, Felix seemed to rush toward her. There was the sound of bodies pressed against the brick wall of the bathroom; there was the sound of kissing, real kissing— the kind of kissing that meant a new year had begun.

And Angie, her heart shattering into a million little pieces, could only make her way to her coat in defeat, grab her keys, and depart.

Apparently, her marriage was over. Felix just hadn't told her yet.

Chapter Two

arie Collins had been a renowned harpist throughout her twenties and early thirties prior to her marriage and subsequent motherhood. When Marie drifted out of the music community (and into daycares, doctor's offices, and gymnastics competitions), she also drifted pretty far out of Angie's realm. When Angie called her on January 8th, fresh off the most horrific conversation of her life— Marie confessed that, much like Angie, she'd just split up from her husband. Sadly, it was nice to connect with a friend who had gone through something similar.

"You're kidding," Angie breathed, genuinely shocked. Marie and her business exec husband had seemed a picture-perfect couple, the sort you didn't question.

"Unfortunately not." Marie's voice was shadowed and gritty, directly contrasting the spunky brightness from her early twenties.

Angie leaned up against the outer brick wall of her apartment complex as Chicago snow fluttered around her, dotting her nose and her cheeks. Upstairs, she could still feel the

sinister darkness of her husband. After days of fights, of listless-
ness, Angie had finally decided to leave him and quit the jazz
band. With one fell swoop, she no longer had her love or her
job.

"You want to come over and talk about it?" Marie asked.

"Well..." Angie's throat tightened. In actuality, she needed
a whole lot more than that. She wanted nothing to do with
Felix, or with the apartment, she'd painstakingly decorated over
the years, wanted nothing to do with the familiar smells and the
sound of Felix practicing the saxophone, and certainly nothing
to do with the piano that beckoned, continually, for her to come
practice it. Perhaps she would never make music again.

"You need somewhere to stay," Marie guessed. "And
wouldn't you know it? I have a guest room with your name
on it."

Apparently, in the wake of Marie's separation and
impending divorce, her husband had rented her an apartment
just west of downtown and a few blocks from his residence.
This, he'd thought, was perfect, as their children were still
teenagers and could easily move back and forth between them
— sleeping at mom's place one weekend and dad's the next.
Because the children were only a few years from university and
could generally care for themselves, Marie and her husband
hadn't bothered with custody conversations. Theirs surrounded
that baseless yet all-important element: money and how much
Marie would get.

"After all," Marie continued as she poured Angie a mug of
hot tea later that afternoon. "I quit my career and raised his
children for years. I haven't so much as blinked at a harp since
then."

Angie wanted to tell Marie how lucky she was that her
husband was the sort of man with a healthy bank account, the
kind she could now dip into in the wake of their separation. She
wanted to point at the apartment walls around them, the safety

there that he'd built for her. Felix and Angie were musicians; they hadn't lived paycheck-to-paycheck, exactly, but they certainly hadn't saved up for any sort of catastrophe. They hadn't saved up for Felix's wandering eye.

"You said she was in your jazz band?" Marie asked as she sat at the kitchen table.

"I've known her for three years," Angie whispered. Her voice cracked at the edges.

"Damn." Marie breathed on her mug of tea to try to cool it.

Angie wondered what it was that had led to Marie and her husband's separation. Had it been his inability to communicate with her any longer or the fact they stopped sharing intimate moments together? She wanted to ask but found the question to be too crass. If Marie wanted to speak about it, that was her prerogative.

Marie showed Angie the guest bedroom, where a queen-sized bed was lined with maroon-colored sheets. An antique mirror gave her a squiggly reflection of a forty-five-year-old woman with sagging weights beneath her eyes and disheveled curly reddish-brown hair, which she'd dyed for the previous seven years. Angie placed her suitcase at the foot of the bed and gazed out at the impossible chill of a Chicago winter's afternoon.

"You can stay as long as you like," Marie assured her from the doorway. "My kids don't hang around at either of our places so much these days. After all those years of taking care of their every need, asking them to keep quiet... now I find myself alone in this empty and quiet apartment."

Angie's heart felt squeezed. She dropped onto the edge of the bed, which bounced beneath her.

"I've shared a bed with Felix every day for the past twenty-three years," she murmured.

Marie nodded. "It takes some time to get used to. At least,

that's what I've read. I'm still too fresh into this to really understand it myself."

"I guess we can figure it out together."

Marie fidgeted. She clearly wanted to head back to whatever she'd been doing prior to Angie's arrival. But before she marched back down the hallway, she asked, "Do you hate him?"

"Felix?"

"Of course."

Angie pressed her lips into a thin line. The question struck her as both odd and understandable at once. She and Marie sat in unknown territory, two soon-to-be-divorcées on a quest for meaning.

"I don't think I could ever hate him," Angie whispered then. "That kind of love doesn't just go away."

Marie dropped her eyes to the carpet. Silence swelled between them.

"I feel terrible, then, for saying that I hate my husband for what he did to us," Marie confessed. "He refused to try to make things work with me. He refused to tell me what was on his mind, and instead, he drifted further and further away from me, from us, and he left me feeling alienated and alone. I don't even know if he ever cheated on me. I've decided it doesn't fully matter. Everything else that he did was so much worse. And now, I ask myself every morning and every night if I'm deserving of love at all."

Angie was surprised at Marie's sudden declaration of her truth. She rushed toward her and draped her arms around Marie as a sob escaped her lips. The two women stood in the shadows of the hallway as Marie's body shook while she sobbed in her arms. Angie realized that she hadn't yet cried, not about Felix and not about the loss of her job. When would those tears come?

Marie stepped back and wiped her sleeve across her cheek

and under her eyes, where mascara and eyeliner had smeared shadows. She looked embarrassed yet youthful, more like the woman Angie had known back in music school.

"I was thinking we could order pizza later," Marie suggested as she tried to contain herself. "God knows that I haven't eaten a proper meal in a few days."

"Sounds good to me," Angie returned with a slight smile.

Marie walked to the kitchen while Angie made her way to the guest bedroom to try to get settled. She removed sweaters, black pants, jeans, skirts, and turtlenecks from her suitcase and lined them in the top two drawers of the dresser. She removed the jeans she'd worn to Marie's and sat in just her underwear and a sweater on the bed, her legs crossed beneath her.

Heavy with devastation and at a complete loss, Angie did something that she hadn't done since New Year's Eve.

She dialed her daughter's number.

Please, Hannah. Please. Answer me. I need you now more than ever before.

Hannah's phone rang six times before it went to voicemail. Angie knew better than to leave one. Nobody checked that sort of thing anymore and besides, Hannah never went anywhere without her phone. Almost assuredly, she'd watched the call come in and counted out the seconds until the hang-up.

Hannah didn't even know about her father and mother's separation. She didn't even know about the affair. In her mind, her mother was just walking around that little apartment she'd left behind in Hyde Park, trying occasionally to reach out to her again.

Angie dropped back to place her head on the pillow behind her. She left her phone on her chest. It would vibrate if Hannah got up the nerve to call her back.

The last time Angie had seen Hannah, Hannah had been half-drunk and stinking of the previous night's party. Angie hadn't told her she planned to stop by Hannah's Logan's

Square apartment. Hannah had called her appearance a "surprise" and then, later, an "ambush." Angie had only wanted to ask Hannah if she wanted to go out to get something to eat, as she'd been in the area meeting with a local jazz club owner. Where had Felix been? Angie wasn't sure any longer.

Hannah's makeup had crusted along her eyes, across her forehead. Angie had sat at her kitchen table and watched her daughter guzzle an entire bottle of water to combat her hangover.

"It's good you're getting all that fun in before classes start," Angie had said.

Hannah had rolled her eyes at that. She'd pressed her fingers to her lips and said, "These lips haven't met a trumpet in quite some time."

"Honey, you know you can't go that long without practicing. The music world is terribly competitive."

Hannah's eyes had glittered. "Maybe I don't want anything to do with the music world, Mom. It's not like it's done much for you over the years."

Angie had tried to rebound their conversation, but Hannah had insisted that Angie leave her alone. Perhaps she'd been ashamed of how far she'd fallen; perhaps she'd just been too hungover to speak. Regardless, one week later, Hannah had written to Felix (not Angie) that she'd dropped out of the University of Chicago "for now" in order to think about where she wanted her life to go.

Back then, Felix hadn't understood Angie's fear and rage around her daughter's decision.

"It's better this way. Better not to waste all that money on something she's not entirely sure she wants to do," Felix had said.

"I think she dropped out of her promising career to party her life away!" Angie had cried.

"Right. Like we didn't do our fair share of partying over the years," Felix had said.

"Yes, but we still stayed in school, Felix. We still got our degrees."

Felix had rolled his eyes expressively, as though certain Angie couldn't fully comprehend the depths of Hannah's emotions. He, the top musician of the house, was always allowed more emotions than Angie. He was allowed to scream and cry. He was allowed to empathize with their twenty-year-old daughter.

Only he was allowed to have an emotional and sexual affair, while Angie had been faithful to the core.

* * *

A week had passed, and then another. It was now the third week of January. Angie fell into a routine at Marie's place, one that didn't resemble her previous life at all. As neither Marie nor Angie could sleep very well, both awoke early in the morning and did a one-hour yoga session via an internet video. They then ground up spinach, strawberries, almond milk, chia seeds, and banana for a nutrient-packed smoothie. Felix would have hated it in every conceivable way.

"You look good," Marie complimented her. "The yoga has done wonders for your arms."

Angie shrugged as she rolled back up her yoga mat. "You look good, too. Really good."

"Thanks, hun," Marie sighed. "I sometimes wonder about that. Nobody's around to appreciate my yoga body. Why don't I just sit around eating Cheetos all the time?"

"We could have a no-yoga, full-Cheeto day if you want to," Angie joked.

Marie shook her head. "If my teenagers come in and find me like that, I couldn't live with myself. I guess it's just an act. I want to convince my teenagers and my husband and myself that I'm good enough to look like this."

Marie had a number of errands to run in downtown Chicago that afternoon. Angie found herself alone at the apartment with very little to do. Lately, her fingers had felt strange and loopy and unused. This was the longest Angie had ever gone without playing the piano. She wasn't entirely sure who she was without the keys.

Was there a way she could separate her love of music from her love for Felix? Or had the two loves become so inextricably linked over the years? She and Felix had performed for thousands and thousands of hours; they'd improvised deep into the night, hunting around for the next track they planned to teach the Lake City Rollers. They'd tried to fill their daughter with a love of music, teaching her blues scale when she was no older than six.

What had it all added up to? Was her life just over, now, at the age of forty-five?

Angie perched at the kitchen table with a fashion magazine spread out before her. She'd never had a terribly great interest in clothing and had always struck out for deals at TJ Max rather than high-end couture. She eyed these fashion models, with their sleek and long torsos, their long legs, and again felt further and further away from herself. The world belonged to women like this.

As Angie had raised Hannah, she'd tried her darnedest to create a sense of self-worth in her daughter. She'd wanted her daughter to look at her reflection and consider how intelligent she was, what a prosperous musician she was, and how strong her stomach was after hours and hours of trumpet performance. She hadn't wanted her to see someone who didn't measure up.

The world always had its way with you, she supposed. It always told you that you were less-than. It showed you that the love of your life will always, always go for the younger woman in the jazz band. It showed you that you'd never look like the women in the magazines.

Angie flung the magazine toward the corner of the room just as her phone buzzed with a call from her stepmother, Janice. What a funny person to call her just then. Janice was probably the vainest woman Angie had ever met— very thin and fashionable, with never a makeup line out of place. She'd married Angie's father at the age of twenty-seven, when Angie had been in her teens, which meant that now, the two women were terribly close in age. Forty-five and sixty-one didn't make a world of difference.

"Hi, Janice." Angie hadn't yet informed her father and stepmother about her divorce. Neither of them had taken much interest in her life over the years, especially after she'd decided to live out her days as a musician with Felix by her side.

"Angela, hello." Janice's voice was icier than usual, yet it quivered at the end as though she struggled to maintain power over herself.

Something strange and sharp pierced Angie's stomach.

Phone calls out of the blue like this never meant anything good, did they? Angie dropped her head to allow her red-tinged curls to fall down the back of the chair.

"I'm terribly sorry to call you like this," Janice started. "But we've had a rather trying few days here in Cincinnati. You see, your father— he suffered a major stroke. And, darling, I hate to tell you this, but it seems that we lost him."

Angie closed her eyes, no longer surprised that tears never rushed forward at the news of this devastation. Perhaps she'd lost all contact with her emotional core.

Her father was dead.

Angie found herself falling through the hoops of things you were meant to ask when such things happened. *When, exactly, had it happened? Had he had any health problems prior to the stroke? When would the visitation and funeral be?*

"It will be good to see you and Hannah again," Janice said softly toward the tail-end of their conversation. "Your father always loved that daughter of yours. He always said she was going to take on the world."

Angie's throat tightened. "Hannah loved her grandfather to bits." She swallowed hurriedly to try to loosen herself up. "I'll see you soon, then, Janice. I'll let you know when I'm on my way."

Chapter Three

Chester Fitzgerald had been a beloved figure of Greater Cincinnati. Over the years, he'd been head of nearly every charity board across the city, volunteered at countless soup kitchens and auctions to raise money for children, and was often called the "unofficial" mayor of Cincinnati, although back in the eighties, he'd tried a run for office which had failed. Throughout her youth, Angie had fallen in the shadows of her father, knowing that she didn't stack up to his expectations for her future. When she'd majored in music and then married Felix, her father hadn't bothered to attend her graduation or her wedding ceremony. She'd wanted to say, "to hell with him" over the years, but something had always held her back. She supposed it was the kindness he'd shown her after Hannah's birth. "Fatherhood was the greatest gift of my life," he'd written her in a letter. "I know you'll find the beauty that I did."

Now, Angela Fitzgerald Montague stood in the foyer of the funeral parlor on Parkcrest Lane and awaited the final hours of the celebration of her father's life. The visitation the previous afternoon had brought thousands upon thousands of Cincinnati residents to the door of the funeral home, so much so that a line had wrapped around the block. Angie's stepmother had wept throughout, leaving Angie to greet the guests and thank them for their kind words.

Hannah, who'd learned of her grandfather's death after finally reading Angie's text message, hadn't bothered to come.

To his credit, Felix had called during the hour after the visitation to check-in. Angie hadn't answered it, but he'd left her a voice message that said:

"Hey, Ang. I know you don't want to talk to me right now. I just want to check in with you about your dad. I know you had complicated emotions about the old guy and I can't imagine how you're feeling right now. Just— um, let me know if you need anything. Anything at all."

Angie wore a clean black dress, a pair of tights, and low heels. She'd tamed her curls as best as she could and allowed them to run down her shoulders and across the top of her back. She glanced at herself in the wall-sized mirror toward the far end of the foyer and saw who she was to the world just then: a grieving daughter smack-dab in middle age, without another family member to show for it.

Janice's heels clacked across the foyer marble. Angie turned to find the widow, just skin and bone and clear blue eyes that seemed to penetrate straight through her. For a couple of years after Chester had married Janice, Janice had asked Angie to call her "Mom." But since Angie's own mother had passed away when she'd been eleven, there was no way in hell Angie would transition that term over. She'd always just been "Janice," and, over time, that had been good enough for the both of them.

"Not long now," Janice whispered. She lifted a wadded-up tissue to the edge of her eye. "I only wish the funeral home could accommodate more guests. So many people want to be here to say goodbye."

Angie sniffed as the funeral director skirted out from the main hall to tell them everything was set and ready for the ceremony. Chester's long-time friend and pastor, lovingly known as Pastor Rick, would give a brief sermon, which would lead up to something Angie dreaded more than anything: words from Chester's only daughter, his only kin. Angie herself.

Angie had stumbled through several drafts of the speech the evening before. She'd slowly gotten through an entire bottle of wine along with it, scribbling out half-understood sentences for herself before wadding up each individual piece of paper and shooting them like baskets into the trashcan. Needless to say, she hadn't a clue what she would say when she got up there. She wasn't entirely sure why she'd agreed to it in the first place.

"Have you heard from Hannah?" Janice asked her then, her brows stitching together as best as they could. Three days ago, she'd decided to get Botox injections to "look her best" for the funeral, which had resulted in a stiff and unemotional face.

"Yes," Angie lied. "She's just so busy with school these days. She really wanted to make it."

"I thought Chester had said something about her dropping out last semester."

Angie locked eyes with her stepmother as she's lied once more. "She's back at it this semester."

"Oh, dear me. That's wonderful to hear. Chester was quite worried about the poor girl. You know how much he loved her."

The words echoed through Angie's skull. *Yes,* she thought now. Chester had loved Hannah. He'd had endless forgiveness for her actions, her dropping out from university and her occasionally reckless partying, which had begun in her teenage years and then affected her university course load to the point of dropout. But Janice didn't need to know more about the rift between Angie and Hannah than she already did. Angie wouldn't tell this woman her soul-crushing truth. She owed her nothing.

* * *

Pastor Rick stood at the pulpit of the funeral home before four-hundred and fifty-seven mourners who had come to grieve the loss of Chester Fitzgerald. Angie sat up front alongside Janice and Janice's two sisters and watched as Janice's younger sister, a woman who'd married a very rich yet very old man who'd died years ago, toyed with her Tiffany bracelet with bright-pink fingernails. Janice had never had many kind words to say about her youngest sister yet had spent the previous thirty minutes weeping on her shoulder. That was family, Angie supposed. Not that she could possibly understand what family truly meant these days.

"Chester and I were dear friends growing up," Pastor Rick began. "So much so that when I wanted to go to seminary, I had to beg him not to spill all my secrets from my wild roots as a young Ohio boy with something to prove. Through those memories, Chester was always right there beside me— driving too fast down country roads and playing guitar deep into the night."

Here, Pastor Rick's eyes glowed with tears.

"When we got a bit older, we both noticed a beautiful change within the other," Pastor Rick continued. "While I studied the Word of God and grew closer to Him, Chester became something of a community-minded man. He was always the first to volunteer at the local charity or donate to the food drive or help out in any way he could."

Here, Pastor Rick's tear-filled eyes found Angie's and held on tight. Angie shifted uncomfortably and dropped her gaze. She'd never known Pastor Rick that well. Throughout her youth, he had wanted to joke with her and play "uncle" in some way, but Angie's distance from her father hadn't allowed her to loosen up. This had made Angie seem stiff and asocial. Very soon, Pastor Rick had given up.

"Watching him become a father to Angela was a beautiful gift as well," Pastor Rick continued, still trying to make eye contact with Angie. "He took to it with all the life and joy you'd imagine a man like Chester to have. He loved his daughter and his wife and his granddaughter, Hannah, to pieces. You couldn't have run into him the past twenty-some years without seeing him brag about his granddaughter or see the sparkle in his eye at just the mention of her name."

Across the funeral home, everyone laughed in recognition. Everyone who was everyone across Cincinnati seemed to know a thing or two about Hannah— seemed to have pride for their Hannah. Not one of them actually knew her. Not one of them could say that she'd glared at them in the eyes and said, *I wish you hadn't been my mother."*

After Pastor Rick finished his speech, he beckoned for Angie to rise and come up to the pulpit. This was the moment Angie had been dreading. She had no idea of what to say. The idea of "speaking from the heart" made her feel devastated, as she hadn't connected her heart with ideas about her father in so long.

Once at the head of the massive collection of grievers, none of whom seemed familiar to her after so many years away from Cincinnati, Angie cleared her throat and moved the microphone toward her mouth. As a result, the microphone screamed, and half of the onlookers smacked their hands over their ears in shock.

"Sorry about that," Angie finally spoke, sounding foolish. After a pause, she added, "I can't imagine what my father might have said about something like that. Probably, something to the tune of, 'Angela, you know better than to talk in public!'"

Angie waited for a moment to allow for the crowd to laugh or sigh with recognition. They did neither. Her stomach pumped with panic.

"But, no. I mean." Sweat pooled at the base of her back. "What I mean is, Chester Fitzgerald was a really terrific man— a man that I so often looked up to. I always wondered where he got the energy to do everything he did. When I was running late for school, he'd always give me a lift without asking any questions. I probably seemed so lazy to him. By that time of the morning, he'd already been to the YMCA for his daily workout and was plotting to help someone in the community. Someone who really needed it."

Angie looked down at the audience, who now nodded with interest, were leaned forward, completely captivated and grateful for these last words from Chester's only living daughter. Angie turned her gaze to the glow of the casket, where a framed photograph of her eighty-five-year-old father— a man who was forty years old when she entered the world— stood, featuring a well-dressed and white-haired man with a mischievous twinkle in his eye. That mischievous twinkle had never been reserved for Angie.

Angie continued on with her speech, making it all up as she went along and lingering perhaps too long on the subject of her daughter, Hannah. Each time she said the word "Hannah," her heart swelled like a bruise right after a hard hit. Would her daughter ever allow her to see her again? Or would she hover just out of reach forever? Sometimes, Angie's anger made her think ridiculous things, like that she and Felix should cancel Angie's cell phone plan, if only so that she had to know what it really felt like to be out there in the wide world alone. But then, in the same thought, she realized that she just couldn't. Canceling the phone plan meant that Hannah would have to get a whole new phone number, one that Angie wouldn't know by heart. That would break her in two.

It seemed against nature itself that Hannah never appeared at the funeral home doors that afternoon. Her name was said upwards of two hundred times as guests approached to give their condolences and ask about Angie's "exciting life in the Windy City." Angie's smile nearly cracked her face open.

"She's doing quite well," Angie heard herself say of Hannah. "She's just been keeping herself busy. She is preparing to take on the world, just like her Grandpa Chester would have wanted."

Chapter Four

Bar Harbor, Maine

Little bright orange carrots were lined up like soldiers on the soft wood of the Acadia Eatery kitchen cutting board. Luke, the Acadia Eatery sous chef, brandished his knife, allowing it to catch the bright light in such a way that it reflected directly into the eyes of Nicole Harvey, the Acadia Eatery's top chef, who had collected herself in a tizzy fit in the corner, perfecting the evening's menu.

"Ahh..." Nicole jumped away from Luke's reflected light, her face lined with annoyance. "Stop that. Do you want me to fire you and hire a new sous chef who actually does his work?"

Luke tittered with laughter, as he knew very well she didn't mean it at all. Anxiety was the name of the game, especially when it came to Friday night at the Acadia Eatery. Nicole had made quite a name for herself at the restaurant, so much so that hungry "foodies" from across New England set their sights on the Keating Inn of Bar Harbor and journeyed from miles around, just to taste her cuisine. She had real, rich talent—one that Luke's own cooking talent could hardly match. But if anything within him yearned for that top chef life, he usually turned those thoughts away. He didn't want all the anxiety, and he certainly wasn't as organized as Nicole Harvey.

"How did it go last night?" Luke asked Nicole as she settled across from him at the kitchen island, positioning her chef's hat.

"Casey looks happier than ever," Nicole said. "Her trip to Barcelona was brilliant."

"The job's going to pan out?"

"It's looking like it," Nicole affirmed. "It warms my heart to see my sister back to her old self. During our twenties, you couldn't get her to stop working."

"That's the thing about the Harvey girls," Luke started. "You've all found your passions, and nobody can keep you away from them— not for long, anyway."

Nicole's eyes sparkled. "Heather knows she's been working too hard lately. But you know how it is when writers get the spark of inspiration. They just have to dig into it before the idea disappears."

"I know, I know." Luke's grin stretched ear-to-ear. He felt strangely like a teenager, all light with feeling for that beautiful Heather Harvey. Their relationship had never been precisely "set in stone," which made his embarrassment even more heightened. What had Heather told her sisters about her feelings for him? Was she ready to run for the hills at any moment? Or would she finally consider making Luke her actual boyfriend?

It wasn't that Luke blamed her. She'd had a very difficult year and a half. It had all begun when her husband, Max, had disappeared on one of his oceanographer adventures. To say that Max had been Heather's "greatest love" was probably an understatement. How could she allow anyone else to fill those shoes? Was Luke even up to such a task? He wasn't sure.

"All relationships are based on communication." Sylvia, the

bartender where Luke was a regular, had expressed this to him repeatedly the past few weeks. Luke took to worrying about Heather around the middle of the second beer, dispelling his sorrows to the woman who'd been his makeshift "mother" there in Bar Harbor over the years. Eventually, she'd all-but smacked him over the head and said, "Listen. If you're not going to talk to Heather about this, then I will."

"I heard you're cooking her up something special after work today, though." Nicole arched an eyebrow in Luke's direction expectantly, wanting him to know that she knew much more than she let on.

Luke blushed yet again and slid a knife through another carrot. "Yeah, yeah. That's the plan."

"Just don't screw up the recipe again," Nicole teased.

"That was one time! One time, and you'll never let me forget it."

"You bet I won't."

* * *

The Friday night rush propelled at Nicole, Luke, and the rest of the kitchen staff, just as it always did, leaving them breathless yet optimistic, eager to laugh and tease one another as they closed up shop. Another top foodie journalist had been in the crowd and had apparently licked his plate clean, which would result in yet another top review regarding Nicole's sinful cooking.

Casey and Abby appeared in the kitchen to congratulate Nicole and Luke on the evening's success. Abby flung her arms around her mother as she cried, "Mom, I don't even know what to say!" Luke understood that Abby and Nicole had had their differences in the past and had only come together as a powerful mother-daughter duo in the previous four months. He could see the ways it made both mother and daughter whole again.

His past as an orphan tossed around from orphanage to various foster homes across Ohio made him appreciate the love of family all the more— even if it sometimes felt like a foreign idea, something he couldn't fully grasp.

Even still, the Harvey sisters had done their darnedest to open their hearts to him.

Perhaps his love for the youngest one wasn't the smartest thing in the world. If there was one thing he'd learned over the years, it was that romantic love wasn't always something you could trust. It felt far more like a teeter-totter, with the power switching from person to person until its inevitable break.

That had been Luke's experience over the years, anyway. He'd hardly dated much since his arrival to Bar Harbor, as everyone knew everyone else, and gossip flung freely through the quaint little houses and grew sour. He didn't want his romantic life to be on display like that. At least, he didn't want that unless it was with someone who actually mattered.

"Casey," Luke called as he removed his chef whites. "Congratulations on the new job over in Spain. You must be so excited."

Casey beamed, looking almost childish. "Thanks a lot, Luke. I really missed Bar Harbor a lot while I was gone. I can't believe I'm even saying that after all those years of promising that I would never come back here again."

"We all say a lot of things, don't we?" Luke joked, cocking an eyebrow.

"You got that right."

Casey had always been the more standoffish of the Harvey girls, at least until Christmas, when everything changed for her. Her on-again, off-again relationship with her husband, had become very much ON, so much so that Grant now spent nearly all of his time in Bar Harbor. Luke had grown to really like the guy, going so far as confiding in him the previous weekend about how much he loved Heather.

"It's not like it's a secret," Grant had told Luke. "You just need to talk to her about it. That's the thing me and Casey recently realized. Our communication was garbage. We had to work on it, or we were doomed."

Everyone seemed to guide him toward this mission. *Tell Heather Harvey how you feel. Otherwise, you'll drive yourself crazy (not to mention everyone else) with your wondering.*

"Are you done for the night?" Nicole asked as Luke sped for the door.

"Yep. The brisket should be just about done."

"Brisket! Our Heather has something to look forward to," Casey said.

"She's been locked in her bedroom for days," Abby offered. "Lucky you! You get to spend time with her."

Luke leaped from the front foyer of the Keating Inn and stepped through the crisp, newly fallen snow en route to his pick-up truck. He paused before getting in to stare out across the soulful dark blue of Frenchman Bay, which caught the sharp edge of the crescent moon in its reflection. Years before, when Luke had driven up to Bar Harbor after a stint in New York City, he'd hardly believed his eyes. Throughout all his years of searching for meaning, for a place where he belonged, it seemed he'd imagined this place. He had never envisioned that it was actually real.

As Luke crept up the driveway between the Keating Inn and the main house, Heather appeared on the front porch in her dark blue peacoat. Her luscious nearly-black locks bounced around her shoulders as she rushed excitedly for him. He got out of his truck as his stomach performed backflips.

Was it absolutely nuts to drop down on one knee here and now and ask this woman to marry him?

But when Heather reached him, she didn't lift her chin, as

she so often had before, to kiss him. Rather, she hugged him and burrowed her head in his chest.

It was strange, terribly strange, especially because Heather and Luke hadn't kissed in quite some time, at that point. But Luke decided to shove off his feelings of foreboding and go ahead with their plans for the evening.

"You okay?" Heather asked as she buckled her seatbelt in the front seat of the truck.

"Of course," he lied. "Just glad to see you. Nicole said you've been hard at work on your next book."

Heather's grin widened. "I fell into a kind of trance, I think. Fleshing out the characters and building this whole new world. It's been such a dream. I haven't managed to forget reality since, well. Since before Max..."

Luke nodded as his lips curved downward. Naturally, her husband's death was at the forefront of her mind at all times. Why had he even thought she'd wanted to kiss him?

If you never talk to her about this, then you'll never know what's in her heart. The thought came from somewhere deep in the depths of his soul— and he sensed the truth of it. Perhaps he had to experience this pain if only to understand the reality of the situation. Perhaps this was the only way through.

Back at his place, Heather, who was accustomed to it, headed to the living room to put a vinyl on the record player. She chose Paul Simon's *Graceland*, which immediately reminded Luke of long-ago days back in NYC when his old roommate had played nothing but "Fifty Ways to Leave Your Lover" until Luke had grown to hate it.

Luke now told Heather that story as he poured them both glasses of wine.

"That's great," Heather smiled brightly. "Did he ever manage to leave his lover?"

"Actually, he did," Luke replied. "And that's where the story gets really interesting. He left her, and then she got engaged to some other guy almost immediately and it almost destroyed him. He ran to her and begged for forgiveness."

Heather's ocean-blue eyes widened to the size of saucers. "You're kidding."

"I really wish I was."

"What happened?"

"She took him back." Luke shrugged. "And then about a year later, they had triplets, and I never really saw them again."

Heather giggled, even as her eyes grew shadowed. "Gosh. Raising twins was hard enough. I can't imagine triplets, all three screaming babies at once. You'd have to be a really strong person."

"Both mentally and physically," Luke added. "Imagine carrying more than one baby at once!"

They sat with their wine as the last of the brisket cooked off. Luke adored listening to the sound of Heather's voice as she prattled on about her recent research for the book and her excitement regarding one of the main characters.

"I really thought she was quieter and less courageous than she turned out to be," Heather offered. "But sometimes, your characters surprise you."

"What do you mean?"

"They suddenly do something that you'd never imagine them to do," Heather said. "It's like they take on a life of their own."

Luke's heart swelled with love for her. His lips parted in preparation. Just do it. Tell her that you've surprised yourself with how much you love her. Tell her that you want no other love but the one you have with her. Tell her...

But before he could begin, Heather burst into an exciting announcement of her own.

"Listen, Luke. I have some news."

Luke's heart banged away with sudden apprehension. What the hell did that mean? Was she headed out of the city and away from him? Had she met someone? Was that why she hadn't wanted to kiss him outside of the truck earlier?

"Okay..." he began.

Heather's smile was electric. Luke willed himself to stop this addiction. He turned his gaze toward the corner as his hands grew clammy with sweat.

"I think I've told you before that one of my main characters is also an orphan," Heather continued. "And it got me thinking about what it meant for me to figure out where I came from, who my mother and father actually were. And that led me to think about— about you, Luke. About how much you've meant to me since I arrived here last year. And how much I really want to help you with your own journey."

Luke bristled at her words. He arched an eyebrow in confusion. "My journey?"

"I've been in contact with the foster care program in Ohio," Heather continued, breathless. "And they've told me that it's entirely possible to discover the birth parents of foster children from the era you were born. I told them a bit about your story, and they said it seems familiar— that they've tracked down parents in similar cases before."

Luke's lips curved toward his chin. He leaned back in his chair, lifted his glass of wine, and swirled the dark red liquid as he contemplated her words. His thoughts were difficult to decipher.

It seemed to him that Heather had gone out of her way to do something he'd told her that he wasn't ready for: find his true family.

And it also seemed that she'd done that at a very opportune time. It was as though she'd known, on some intuitive level, that Luke wanted to confess his love to her that night. Her only tactic, it seemed, was to distract him with the darkest crater in his heart.

Ten days after his birth, he'd been dropped off at an

orphanage. Although he and Heather had both grown up without the parents who'd created them, their story was inherently different. Heather had grown up loved and adored, with two sisters who stood by her side even today. Luke had grown up with nothing.

It was enough to enrage him, the fact that she thought she understood his story but never really could.

"Heather," he began, even as she spoke over him.

"I was thinking that we could go there together," she suggested. "Fly to Ohio and really figure this out. We can pore over old documents the way we did with my story. We can—"

"What can we do, Heather? Make peace with a past that I ran away from a long time ago? And for what reason, exactly?" Luke's voice was deep, his agitation ringing through. "Is it just so you can feel better about the fact that you don't—"

The fact that you don't love me back? This was what Luke really wanted to say. But he knew, once he verbalized this, he could never take his words back. If she agreed? If she told him that she didn't love him and never could? He wasn't sure he could recover.

What a monstrous thing it was, getting older and sadder and more alone. What a monstrous thing it was to fall in love. He gaped at her as the silence swelled between them.

"I just can't believe you went behind my back to do this," he finally scoffed. "I told you I wasn't ready, Heather. I told you that I didn't want this."

Heather's eyes filled with tears. She muttered something with disbelief and bolted for the doorway, where she'd hung her coat. In a rush, she shoved her arms through the sleeves.

"Heather! Where are you going? It's freezing outside."

But already, Heather rushed into the dark and frigid night. Luke was flabbergasted. He felt like a rock, altogether too heavy on his chair. He half-expected Heather to come back in and at least demand a ride back to the Keating House. It was more than a mile back to the Keating property— an impossible feat on this winter night.

"Heather?" Luke cried as he raced toward the door. How long had it been since she'd rushed from his dining room table? Thirty seconds? Two minutes? His head spun with rage and sorrow, making him disoriented. If someone had told him the past couple of minutes hadn't happened, he would have believed them.

When he reached the doorway, however, he spotted Heather down by the road, leaping into a dark car he didn't recognize. Without putting back on his boots, Luke flew down the steps of his coastal house and rushed for the vehicle. But before he got there, the car sped out of sight. The back window illustrated an advertisement for a car service. Heather had acted as quickly as possible to run away from his world.

Luke wore only his jeans, a flannel shirt, with a pair of wool socks. He stood in seven inches of snow as the wetness and chill crept through the thick wool and between his toes. The car Heather had called to pick her up soon disappeared in the late-night fog.

She was gone. And he hadn't been able to tell her the enormous feelings that made his heart grow with longing. Perhaps she would never forgive him for acting so angrily.

He turned on his heel and made his way back toward the house, where he sat and removed his snow-filled socks and stared at the black night sky above. Why was he so unwilling to face his past? And had his fear of his past swallowed his potential future whole?

Chapter Five

Cincinnati, OH

Chester Fitzgerald's lawyer was the first to call her father's will "elaborate."

"You can imagine," the lawyer, Scott Walker, said as Angie and Janice sat down with him several days after the funeral. "He wanted to leave a little something for everyone across Cincinnati. Naturally, he made sure to take care of his own. That means the two of you, plus his granddaughter. He loved that girl so much."

For about the millionth time, Angie's heart shattered. "Thank you for meeting us today."

"Of course," Scott returned. "I hated to hear that he left us. Eighty-five isn't such a bad time to go, I suppose. He lived a full life."

"Very full," Janice agreed as she folded her hands primly across her lap. "The most generous man I ever met."

"When was it you met him?" Scott Walker asked Janice as he assembled the will before him, tilting his head.

"I was thirteen," Angie interjected, as though it was her

story to tell. When her father had met and married Janice, Angie had sworn never to look her father in the eye again. She'd been one broody teenager, that was sure.

"He was terribly broken after everything that had happened to him," Janice whispered, almost swooning.

Angie knew that Janice now referred to the death of her mother. It was as though she didn't want to say her mother's name.

"But you two took care of one another," Scott Walker finished, as though Angie's relation to this story mattered very little.

"We did," Janice breathed.

"Well. Again, Janice, I'm terribly sorry for your loss," Scott continued. "And I want to assure you, yet again, that Chester made sure your future is easy and clear."

Scott Walker spent the following twenty minutes illustrating this future for Janice. He spoke about the retirement home that Janice and Chester had picked out for themselves and how that space would now be set aside for Janice alone if she still wanted it.

"Oh, I really do," Janice said.

"Very well. There is a fund set aside for your moving costs," Scott Walker continued.

"We've already started to go through the house," Angie interjected.

"I imagine it will be very difficult to parse through everything and decide what to keep and what to give away," Scott Walker said knowingly.

"Terribly hard," Janice whispered.

"You'll find a way," Scott assured them. "How wonderful that your daughter is here to help you with everything."

Janice cast Angie a doubtful look. Angie matched her doubt right back. Did Scott sense love between them that they couldn't feel?

Scott then moved on to Angie. He disclosed the enormous sum that Chester Fitzgerald had left for her, a number that nearly sent Angie to her knees. Never, in a million years, had she thought that Chester Fitzgerald would leave her more than a couple of pennies to rub together.

She would be okay.

Actually, despite her divorce and her daughter's refusal to speak to her ever again, she would be okay.

It seemed outside the bounds of reason.

"Thank you," Angie gasped, not knowing what else to say.

"Thank your father," Janice added, her voice tart.

Angie wanted to roll her eyes, but she kept that sentiment to herself. This was life-altering.

"And finally, when it comes to family, we arrive at the stipulations regarding Hannah's portion of the will," Scott Walker continued.

Angie's ears perked up. "Stipulations?"

"Yes. You see, Mr. Fitzgerald was quite saddened by his granddaughter's departure from university. He's stated clearly in the will that the money he's left for Hannah Montague shall only be retrievable by said Hannah Montague, should she either achieve her Bachelor's degree or turn thirty years old. Whichever happens first."

"Oh, but that's..." Janice piped up, remembering the lie Angie had told her about Hannah returning to school.

But Angie interjected. "That seems just fine with me, Mr. Walker."

Janice gave her a knowing look. Perhaps it was understood that the two of them couldn't tell one another anything. Perhaps it was understood that lies were commonplace between them.

* * *

An hour later, Janice and Angie arrived back at the three-story downtown house. One with architecture that spoke of a beautiful old-world Cincinnati, one that didn't relate at all to the new glass-filled sky-rise apartment buildings and craft beer bars. Angie had grown up in this house.

A walk up the porch steps brought the same strange gloom of previous eras. Angie's stomach clenched with fear. Normally, Chester Fitzgerald awaited her on the other side of that huge front door. Normally, he would cast his judgmental questions her way, ready to point to her lackluster degree and her small music wages as reasons enough that she was a failure. Now, he was dead.

Angie suggested that she and Janice order pizza. She half-expected the older woman to scoff at the idea. But instead, Janice said, "That sounds nice, honey. Can you call them?"

Angie dialed the downtown pizza joint three blocks south of the house. She ordered a cheese-only (Janice's request) and a small Hawaiian pizza for herself, which had been her favorite as a kid. Her father had said the combination was "sacrilegious," but her mother had adored it. "Nothing beats this!" she'd said excitedly before gobbling each pineapple-filled slice alongside Angie.

Years ago, Hannah had finally asked Angie how Angie's mother had died. When Angie had said, "breast cancer," Hannah had looked stricken and begged her mom to get more frequent check-ups. Angie had acquiesced. Since then, she'd gone once per year for a mammogram. She didn't want to leave her daughter behind— not the way her mother had left her. Her death had shattered her world.

Angie walked the familiar blocks to pick up the pizza. There, she paid with a twenty-dollar bill and thought, yet again, about the money her father had left her. It was a Godsend. She could find her own apartment in Chicago. She could even form her own jazz ensemble if she wanted to.

An empty apartment. A jazz ensemble without Felix at the helm.

Would it break her? Or would it make her feel complete?

Back at her childhood home, Angie and Janice sat on opposite sides of the kitchen table and considered their pizzas.

"Pineapple on pizza? I don't understand." Janice took a delicate bite at the end of her pizza slice and then put the greasy triangle back down again.

Angie wanted to say, *"you would never understand."* But she held it back. Instead, she said, "I think it's pretty clever what Dad put in his will. About Hannah, I mean."

Janice nodded. Her eyes grew shadowed. "Life is happening to her, isn't it?"

Angie's throat tightened. She could hardly believe how astute her stepmother was. It was a rare thing.

Janice finished one slice of pizza and then placed the rest of the box in the fridge for later. It was nearly eight-thirty, and she stretched her arms over her head as a yawn ran over her face. Angie was grateful. They'd spent the entire day together, poring over documents, reading the will, and deciding what to do with some of her father's stuff. There was still more to do in the morning.

"Good night, honey," Janice murmured. "Thank you for your help today. Your father would be so grateful."

"Sleep well, Janice," Angie whispered. "See you in the morning."

Angie's stomach refused more pizza halfway through the second slice. It was sinful, really, to leave all this pizza to grow chilly and stale, especially since the gooey, fatty cheese and the sharp pineapple flavor reminded Angie, so much of her mother.

Sleep would elude her for several hours more, she knew. Exhausted yet strung-out, Angie tip-toed toward her father's study to go over more documents and get a head start on tomorrow's work. Her father had maybe fifty manila folders, stacked one on top of the other, and only about half of them were labeled.

Angie got to work, portioning out files into TRASH, MAYBE, LAWYER, and KEEP. The lawyer ones, obviously, seemed pertinent to the lawyer's responsibilities to her father; the maybe pile was more of an "I don't know" pile, while the trash and the keep were self-explanatory. Naturally, the "keep" pile was the smallest of them all. You just had to make peace with getting rid of stuff. Angie knew that now.

Old documents, signed from the seventies. Old photographs of people she'd never seen before. There was a letter written from her mother from before Angie herself had been born, and the sight of her mother's handwriting nearly ripped Angie in two. She read over it twice, folded it up, and then slipped it carefully into a free envelope, one that Angie had reserved for herself. Janice didn't need to know about it.

Around eleven at night, Angie found a crumpled and water-stained envelope that had been sealed, unlike the others. It wasn't labeled. Angie ripped through the top to find several yellowed pieces of paper. She eased them from the belly of the folder, prepared for another round of old documents and signatures from people who'd died long ago.

But instead, she found something that blew her away.

ADOPTION AGREEMENT BETWEEN THE STATE OF OHIO AND CHESTER AND HANNAH FITZGERALD

The words were typed at the top with a typewriter. It was chilling to see her mother's name there. Hannah Fitzgerald. The woman she'd named her own daughter after— the ghost of Angie's life.

But adoption? What did this mean?

Angie's hands quivered as she forced herself to read.

Angela Barrington - Born November 12, 1976

Adoption - March 17, 1978

Beneath the words, both Chester and Hannah Fitzgerald had signed their names, sealing the deal between them and the state of Ohio.

Angie's jaw dropped.

Adopted? She leaped from the desk chair and rushed toward the window of the study, where she opened the windows as quickly as she could to inhale chilly yet fresh air. How was this possible? Every memory she had from her youth existed within the walls of this house. There was no "her" without Hannah and Chester Fitzgerald.

But according to this document, her parents had never been Chester and Hannah Fitzgerald at all.

In fact, she'd been a year and a half old before she'd entered the door of this gorgeous old-world downtown Cincinnati home.

Chapter Six

Bar Harbor, Maine

Luke wasn't one to call in sick to work, not even due to this impossible level of shame he now experienced. He took his boots off in the foyer of the Keating Inn and lifted his chin to greet Abby, who stood at the front desk, chipper as ever. Her eyes told him what he needed to know: everyone in the family already knew that he and Heather had had some sort of disagreement. They were shadowed and strange. Even her "Good morning!" sounded a bit forced, as though she'd practiced it before he'd entered.

Luke entered the kitchen before anyone else and set to work on lunch prep. Luckily, he had to get through the lunch rush and prepare for dinner and then he was home free. That meant six hours of this horrific, gut-busting public pain— then he could go on home and be in pain in peace.

Nicole did her best to act ordinary. She teased him about this and that, told him he wasn't chopping quickly enough, and then highlighted the specifics of the lunch menu. She then told him he could head home early, around four, saying, "I can prep for once, goodness gracious. It takes my mind off all the hard hours ahead anyway."

Luke was grateful for her kindness. He mumbled thanks and then shot back out into the chilly breeze of January. He tried his best not to glance toward the main Keating House and leaped into his truck. As he eased down the driveway, he spotted someone walking from the Keating House to the Keating Inn. With a jolt of both disappointment and excitement, he realized it was Casey, not Heather.

Perhaps Heather would do her best to avoid him for the rest of the time, as well.

What a waste it all was.

Luke willed away the hours back at his place. He sat on the floor of the living room and listened to the waves rush in off Frenchman Bay. When he'd first purchased this old place five years before, he'd needed a loan, and Joseph Keating, the Harvey girls' uncle, had been the first to step in to tell the bank that Luke was "a-okay." Luke had never felt he could repay Joe for all he'd done for him. He'd given him his first sense of belonging to some kind of family. He'd given him that job in the kitchen. He'd taught him all he knew.

Luke forced himself through the next three days. It was like an out-of-body experience. He felt himself speak to Nicole, asking questions about the set menu for the night; he felt himself laughing at an online video Abby showed him, so much so that tears streamed from his eyes. Moments after, he had no idea what the video had been about. It was all gone.

On the third day, Luke again got out of work at the Keating Inn around four-thirty. This left a crater of an afternoon and evening before him. Exhausted of his time back in his big house alone, he instead drove his truck to the downtown bar, a place of dark mahogany wood and the television blaring all kinds of sports, and local dwellers always searching for their next light beer and their next laugh. Joseph Keating had introduced Luke to the place years before, and since then, the head bartender, Sylvia, had kind of adopted Luke as her own. She'd watched him since the Harvey girls' arrival, noting the shift in his demeanor. "Your eyes tell me you're in love," she'd told him once. "And I don't think it's going to be easy on you, is it?"

Now, Luke kicked off the snow from his boots at the doorway of the establishment. As it was still early, only a couple of barflies sat on stools, their elbows propped up on the wooden bar. Sylvia, just a skinny little woman of five-foot-nothing, walked around the bar and flailed her arms skyward to hug him.

"Luke! Where have you been all my life?"

Sylvia set him up at the far end of the bar with a freshly-poured pint and a bowl of peanuts. Her green eyes glittered as they found his.

"You're in early today," she said finally. "No dinner up at the Acadia Eatery?"

Luke shrugged. "I worked lunch."

Sylvia rapped her knuckles on the bar top and said, "Luke, I've known you for years now. When people ask me if I've got a kid, my stupid brain always thinks of you. Call it mother's intuition. Call it whatever you like. But I gotta know what's on your mind. What's making you look like the saddest dog in all the land?"

Luke dropped his face into his outstretched palms. "Sylvia, I think I really messed up this time."

Sylvia placed her delicate hand on his broad shoulder. "It's about that girl, isn't it? The youngest Harvey?"

Luke nodded into his hands, praying that nobody else at the bar paid him any mind. They were just barflies with nothing else to do. Probably, they had little-to-no care in the world for Luke's silly romantic disputes.

Sylvia poured herself a sliver of whiskey and then leaped

up onto the stool beside Luke. She took a dramatic shot and then placed the empty glass back on the counter.

"Spit it out, Luke. The sooner, the better. I'll help you through this. After twenty-plus years working in a bar, I have a degree in therapy."

Luke laughed inwardly but pressed on, describing the events of the previous few months and the dimensions of his love for Heather. "I've never felt this way before," he breathed, conscious of how lame he sounded. "But when I planned to tell her the truth, it's like she knew I wanted to, and she jumped out of the way of my feelings. Instead, she said that she made contact with the foster care program in Ohio. She wants to go there together and track down my real parents. I was flabbergasted. I've told her so many times over the past few months that I'm not ready to open up that part of my life just yet. That my family is here in Bar Harbor."

Sylvia listened intently. Halfway through his story, she poured herself another sliver-shot of whiskey and sipped it as wrinkles formed between her eyebrows.

"I left the Midwest on purpose," Luke finished. "It's a terrible place of regret and loneliness for me. Bar Harbor is my home. And it seemed to only get better and better over the years, until now when I actually thought..."

"That you wanted to settle down with someone," Sylvia finished.

"I know how stupid it sounds."

"It's not stupid to want to build something with someone," Sylvia affirmed. "It's the most natural thing in the world, at least for most people. And the fact that you grew up without stability and love, yet you still want to build it with someone? That's just about the most beautiful thing in the world. You were given the ashes from a fire, yet you still want to build the house back up."

Luke flared his nostrils. His beer was long-finished. Sylvia leaped up to pour him another as a group of drinkers hustled into the bar and turned on the jukebox. This left Luke alone with his thoughts for nearly a half-hour as Sylvia scrambled to take everyone's orders. It wasn't a pleasant place, his head.

Several hours later, after another few pep talks from Sylvia and another several beers, Luke grabbed his coat and stumbled into the snow, which was illuminated by the moon above. He found himself dialing her number, the only number that mattered. The phone rang out through the night. Three rings, then four, then five. Just when he thought it would take him directly to voicemail, a familiar voice answered.

"Hello?" It wasn't Heather. Rather, it was Kristine— one of Heather's twins, both of whom lived in New York City.

"Kristine, hey." Luke was so surprised that he nearly dropped his phone into the snow.

Wherever Kristine had answered Heather's phone, it was extremely loud. A roar of conversation brewed behind the phone.

"Luke? I can't really hear you!" Kristine called.

"Where are you?" Luke called, slurring his words together.

"Luke? Mom's in the bathroom. Can I have her call you back when we leave?"

Luke's heart pounded wildly, then leaped into his throat. He blinked up at the moon as devastation snaked around his knees and threatened to take him to the ground.

"That's fine," Luke finally replied.

"What?" Kristine returned. "I'll just have her call you. Sorry, I can't hear you."

The call ended abruptly as Luke gaped at the dark screen. It seemed clear: Heather had left Bar Harbor for New York City. Despite his interactions with Casey, Abby, and Nicole over the previous several days, not a single one had mentioned Heather's departure. Did this mean that she'd told them to keep it a secret?

God, it felt so wrong. Luke felt like a timid creature with his arms wide open to a love that wasn't there to welcome him back in return. This abandonment sizzled through him, a reminder of all his previous abandonments.

He dropped himself against the side brick wall. A sob escaped his lips, but he soon shoved it into his belly. He couldn't be that middle-aged guy weeping outside a bar in the snow.

Perhaps Heather had decided that Bar Harbor wasn't meant for her, after all. He would have to understand that. With her husband gone, it stood to reason that she'd want to live closer to her daughters. New York City had more of a literary community as well, which meant that Heather would have people to speak to about her craft. When she spoke excitedly about writing with Luke, all Luke could do was smile. He'd never strung more than a text message together. Cooking was his love language.

Luke lifted his phone to scribe a text now, wanting to leave Heather with his sentiment, even if she couldn't hear his voice. Liquid courage led him to type out:

LUKE: I miss you. And I'm sor...

But before he could finish, his phone dinged and began to turn off. He'd let the battery die out. He cursed himself, cursed technology, and then cursed New York City itself before he shoved his phone into his back pocket and retreated back into the bar.

Chapter Seven

Angie entered a kind of stupor over the next several days. The adoption paperwork, signed by the people she'd assumed were her mother and father for her entire life, was proof that everything was not as it seemed. Inappropriate assumptions were the themes of the year. She'd assumed her marriage was stable, happy, if slightly boring. She'd assumed her career as a jazz pianist wasn't going anywhere. She'd assumed her relationship with Hannah would be forever kind and considerate and warm. It was nearly time to quit assuming, she supposed.

Angie continued to tear through her father's house with a zeal that she'd never experienced. She mopped the bathrooms, scrubbed the toilets and sinks, went through the rest of his documents, and divided up the antique dining wear, most of which would go to Janice. Janice commented several times that Angie was the perfect creature to have around during these sorrowful days. "You use your sadness for handwork. I wish I could say the same about myself."

Angie wanted to scream back at her that she felt like a ship without a harbor. But instead, she muttered something and scuttled back into the office for more organization. She felt like a ghost.

Finally, three days after Angie's discovery, she sat across from Janice, who nibbled at the saddest-looking salad Angie had ever seen. As Janice crunched on a white onion, Angie placed the folder on the table between them.

"What's that?" Janice asked.

"I found this in Dad's study," Angie breathed. She removed the documents and lined them up for Janice to see.

Janice flinched at the sight of Chester and Hannah Fitzgerald's names listed together. She had always been extremely jealous of Angie's mother, even in death, it seemed.

"My goodness." Janice breathed. She dropped her fork into her salad bowl and lifted the adoption papers toward her bifocals. "Adopted?" Her eyes nearly bugged out of her head.

"It seems so."

Janice's eyes filled with tears as the silence brewed between them.

"Did he ever mention this to you?" Angie locked eyes with her stepmother.

Janice shook her head violently. "No. Never..." She sniffled and then added, "I have to believe that he didn't want to brag about this commitment he made. He was never one to go on and on about his good deeds."

Angie's heart felt like someone had used it as a punching bag. Naturally, Janice was hurt that her husband of thirty years hadn't bothered to inform her about this huge, secretive element of his life. Instead of being honest about her feelings, she'd decided to use it as another way to mythologize him into greatness.

"You know that I didn't meet your father until you were thirteen years old," Janice told her, as though Angie needed a refresher course on her own life story.

Angie bristled. "I just can't figure out why he would never have said something."

"He was such a generous man," Janice whispered. "Always so willing to go above and beyond for others. I imagine that your mother was the same way."

"But that's the thing," Angie added flatly. "She wasn't my mother, was she? Hannah and Chester adopted me, which means that my biological parents are out there somewhere. I belong to another group of people. I..."

What she wanted to say, maybe, was that she didn't want to belong to this current family— one made up of only herself and Janice in this house in downtown Cincinnati.

"Maybe he kept some kind of diary," Angie suggested.

Janice shook her head. "He was never one for anything like that. I've never come across a single journal entry."

"What about my mother?"

"I suppose there might have been something years and years ago," Janice replied, furrowing her brow. "But darling, we had to clear all that out so that I could move in."

Angie's heart swelled with anger. It wasn't like she was surprised. Janice had forced her way into Angie and Chester's life and become every bit the sort of woman Chester Fitzgerald was supposed to be married to. In Chester's eyes, Angie had been nothing more than a girl from the wrong side of the tracks. She'd been yet another little girl who'd "needed" his wealth, intellect, and guidance.

This made her decision to go to music school and marry Felix all the more powerful. Chester hadn't been able to morph Angie into the daughter he'd wanted her to be. Perhaps, in a sense, Hannah had been his last hope.

Chapter Eight

The downtown Cincinnati public records office kept hours that indicated the sleepy Midwestern city didn't have much care at all for important documents. Mondays and Tuesdays, the place was open from nine to twelve and Wednesdays and Thursdays, it was open from ten to one. This meant that when Angie planned to visit the records office the day after her conversation with Janice, she missed the office hours by a full, frustrating hour. The following day, she arrived at nine, only to wait around for an hour before being let in. It was enough to make her head spin.

The woman at the front desk of the records office had adult braces and wore a lime green turtleneck. She typed an email hurriedly as Angie arranged herself at the counter. When the woman lifted her eyes to Angie's, she asked, "How can I help you?" in a way that suggested that she really didn't want to help Angie at all.

Angie showed the woman the adoption papers she'd discovered in her father's study. The woman's smile widened in familiarity.

"You're Chester Fitzgerald's daughter!" she cried.

"I'm not sure, to be honest with you," Angie replied, pointing to the adoption paperwork.

The woman's eyes grew shadowed. "Chester was such a marvelous pillar of this community. He helped out at the local children's drive with me about once a week. And he always had a kind word and a joke for me. It must have been just a joy to be raised by him!"

Angie's nostrils flared. "I'd like to know if there's any listing of the people he adopted me from."

"You know what we say at my church?" the woman said, stepping up tentatively from her desk. "We say that God has a plan for all of us. And it seems like God's plan for Chester Fitzgerald to raise you was the right one."

Chester Fitzgerald hadn't said a kind word to Angie since her early childhood. Angie thought about pointing this fact out to the stranger before her but held it back.

"God does have a plan," Angie said instead, hopeful that this would push her to find the file she so needed.

Satisfied, the woman disappeared for a few minutes and then reappeared with an ancient-looking folder, yellowed and crumpled, as though it had been through a storm. The woman flipped the folder open to reveal several photocopies of various documents, including two photocopies of very old driver's licenses. The woman flipped the driver's license around for Angie to see.

It felt strange to share this very intimate moment in Angie's life with this stranger.

But as she gazed down at the two people on these driver's licenses, Angie's heart thumped with recognition.

GLENN BARRINGTON - BORN JULY 13, 1952

WENDY BARRINGTON - BORN APRIL 13, 1956

The photocopies were black and white, but the images were stark, allowing sight of a thin-faced woman with large glowing eyes and a sorrowful smile. There was something about her face, something that related to both Angie and Hannah's faces. The photograph itself was nearly identical to Angie's university ID from twenty-five years before.

"Wow..." Angie whispered.

"I see a resemblance," the stranger before her offered, like some kind of gift.

That moment, the public records office's phone blared. The stranger leaped for it, grateful for something to do, as Angie tried to pore over the rest of the documents within the folder.

"That's right. We close at one," the stranger told the person on the phone. "But I can set aside those documents for you, so it's easy to pick them up. What did you say the name was again?"

Angie's heart pumped as the woman at the front desk turned her back toward her. Angie hadn't the strength to go through these documents just then. She didn't want to do it in the shadow of this strange woman, there at the public records office. This was a very intimate moment of her life.

As the woman at the desk laughed at something the person on the other line said, Angie placed the folder delicately into her purse, turned on her heel, then raced out of the office. Behind her, the woman at the front desk cackled, still on the phone and probably losing all memory of the girl who'd wanted records on Chester Fitzgerald's long-ago adoption. Who else in the world would want to look at this file, anyway? It clearly hadn't been touched by sunlight in forty-five years.

Angie walked back to the house she'd grown up in. The folder in her purse seemed overly heavy, as though aware of the role it played in Angie's existence. Back inside, she found Janice and her sisters sipping tea and speaking in low voices. Angie waved hello to them but quickly leaped up the staircase to the room she now slept in, the one that had once been her own.

Once there, she sat cross-legged on the floor and tried to drum up the courage to go over the documents, to learn more. But before she could flip through, her phone rang. It was Felix.

Perhaps because she felt lonelier in her world than ever before, Angie answered it. Felix had been her everything for twenty-three years. Maybe he could listen to this newfound situation and lend advice. Maybe he, above everyone, could understand.

"Hi."

"Hey, Ang. Happy you answered."

Angie's heart crackled at the edges. The sound of his voice was almost too much to bear. This was still the man she loved. He was still her everything.

"What's up, Felix?" She sniffled. In the background of the phone, a recording of a jazz band could be heard very faintly.

"Gosh, it's hard to talk about this. Especially since I know you're going through so much down there."

"Just tell me, Felix."

"I wanted to let you know that I've found a divorce lawyer," Felix replied.

"I see." Tears pooled in her eyes, but she didn't allow them to fall.

"I guess you probably haven't had much time to look for one of your own."

"You guessed right, Felix."

Again, silence except for the jazz band in the background. Angie cleared her throat.

"What's that recording?"

"Oh, that?" Felix's voice was jagged. It sounded like he moved his head from the speaker to say something to someone else. It sounded like: *"Hey, can you turn that off? I told you, this is important."*

"What was it, Felix?" Angie asked after the music was turned off.

"Oh, just a new recording we made this week," Felix said flippantly.

Angie's throat tightened. "You found a new pianist."

Again, silence.

"You can tell me, Felix," Angie urged him. "I'm a big girl."

Felix guffawed. "Yes, we did. We're just trying her out for now. We recorded with her last week."

"It doesn't sound too bad," Angie offered, feeling just about two inches tall.

"It's not," Felix returned, which added insult to the already horrendous phone call.

This time, Angie's tears slid down from her eyes. She closed them tightly as a way to keep herself in check.

"I can't really talk right now, Felix," Angie told him, remembering the adoption paperwork before her and all the secrets she'd never known.

"Have you talked to Hannah at all?" Felix asked. "I've tried to get ahold of her this week, but she's avoiding my calls left and right. She texted me once to tell me she knows about the divorce. I'm not sure who told her."

A sharp chill radiated up Angie's spine. Gossip had its way of getting through Chicago, but who was Hannah still in communication with? Someone from the music community? And what had been her reaction to the divorce?

Still, Angie didn't want to discuss it with Felix. Not now.

"She doesn't want anything to do with us right now," Angie breathed. "I can't say I blame her."

Then, Angie did something she'd never envisioned herself to do in a million years.

She hung up on Felix.

After that, Angie sat like a shadow on the floor of her childhood bedroom. The facts of her current existence were messed up. When she returned her attention to the papers, Felix texted her to say:

FELIX: Real mature.

But instead of texting Felix back, Angie was suddenly awash with a new idea— one that seemed both inspirational and cruel. With her phone still lifted, she brought up Hannah's phone number and typed in a text.

ANGIE: We need to talk about the money that was left for you in your grandfather's will.

She sent it without adding any additional *I love you* or *I miss you*. It was clear those sentiments didn't work on Hannah any longer.

It felt as though Angie had just dropped a bomb over her daughter's life. One thing was for sure: whatever crap job Hannah worked at now wasn't easy on the bills. The concept of money was probably never far from her mind.

One hour later, Hannah texted her mother back for the first time in over six months.

HANNAH: When will you be back in Chicago?

Chapter Nine

Bar Harbor, Maine

Heavy with disbelief and fear, Luke hailed a cab outside of the Bar Harbor bar and told the driver, "The Keating House." The driver greeted him warmly. Apparently, the two had met and had an interesting chat on the night of the fundraiser that was held at the Keating Inn the previous October, around the time they'd thought the Snow family would kick them off the property. Luke had no memory of the conversation at all but managed to fake his way through it, nodding and smiling as the man spoke.

"And then that little Snow girl stole your boat!" he said. "I couldn't believe that. Did you end up pressing charges?"

Luke shook his head, catching the reflection of his tortured-looking face in the glass of the back window. "I know what it's like to be young and confused," he told the driver.

Heck, he thought. *I know what it's like to be old and confused. I don't know if I've had a moment of clarity in my entire life.*

The driver dropped him at the end of the Keating House

driveway. There, Luke stumbled up toward the glowing orange light of the warm family home. He'd spent Thanksgiving and Christmas and New Year at this very house— often with his arms wrapped tightly around Heather's waist as they swayed to holiday songs. Where had those happy times gone?

When Luke reached the porch, he attempted to collect himself. He swept his hair behind his ears, righted his posture, and then corrected the buttons on his shirt. He'd come all the way to the Keating House; it was time he followed through on why. He lifted his knuckles to the door and knocked, feeling like a stranger.

There was the thudding sound of many footsteps, all headed for the front door. Perhaps they expected someone that night, someone who wasn't Luke. After a moment of fear, Grant opened the door to discover Luke out in the frigid air. His face broke into a confused yet happy grin.

"Luke! Come on in." Grant wrapped his hand around Luke's sturdy shoulder and guided him into the foyer.

Abby hopped out from behind the couch to wave at him. Beside her, Casey gave a little wave. They seemed in the middle of one of those home improvement shows. Luke had frequently asked them, "Aren't all these shows all the same?" To that, they'd just told him he couldn't possibly understand.

"Can I get you something? Coffee? A beer?" Grant asked, his voice booming out confidently. A little more than a month before this, Casey hadn't allowed Grant within a mile of the house. Now, he acted like he owned the place.

"Maybe a coffee." Luke finally answered, his voice weak.

Abby's and Casey's eyes grew curious.

"What's wrong, Luke?" Casey asked, jumping up from the couch to follow Grant and Luke into the kitchen. "Is everything okay?" He could sense that she wanted to get closer to him to smell his breath.

In reality, he'd only had a couple of drinks, nothing more.

He just hadn't eaten properly in a few days. That was the worst of it. He was losing steam.

Luke sat at the kitchen table for perhaps the hundredth time. Part of him could make up a story that Heather was only upstairs, putting on the last of her makeup. Grant began to brew a pot of coffee and chatted about his recent trip to Montana, where his brother was in the midst of a long-time-coming divorce. He no longer traveled as often for work and planned to help out at the Keating Inn more often, making it even more of a family business than ever before. Casey even had plans to build a new house on the Keating Property. It would be a proper Keating community— probably one that Luke wouldn't be entirely welcomed in, providing that Heather ever returned.

With a mug of steaming coffee before him, Luke finally found his voice.

"Why did she leave?" His voice cracked with disbelief.

Grant and Casey exchanged worried glances. Abby appeared in the doorway of the kitchen, her face pale.

"You mean, Aunt Heather didn't tell you?" Abby asked.

"I'm surprised about that, too," Casey added softly.

Luke's lips parted in surprise. Since his and Heather's fight, he'd felt a cold wave from the Keating/Harvey clan, as though they'd collectively decided he wasn't good enough for them. Apparently, he'd made all that up in his head.

"She didn't tell you...?"

Casey shook her head. "She didn't tell us anything."

Luke dropped his chin to his chest. This was peculiar indeed.

"She's in New York City," Abby blurted out. "Her book was optioned for a movie deal, but she was on the fence on whether she would accept or not. Kristine and Bella finally convinced her to accept the offer. It's a deal of a lifetime. She's set to appear on a talk show tomorrow at five-thirty to talk about her process adapting the book into a screenplay."

Luke was genuinely shocked. He wasn't sure what to make of this, either. He'd thought, selfishly, that she had wanted to run away to the city to get away from him. Instead, she had a huge career opportunity. This seemed more in line with her forgetting his name forever. A whole future awaited her, one without him in it.

"Wow. I'm so proud of her," he heard himself say. "Really."

"We can't wait to watch her," Casey told him. "You should come over."

"We have a whole list of snacks planned for the occasion," Abby added.

"I'm sure you do," Luke tried to joke. "You wouldn't be Harvey girls if you didn't have your snacks lined up."

Although Luke's place was a little more than a mile through the snow and chill, Luke opted to walk back home. Grant nearly tried to fling him into his vehicle, but Luke resisted, telling him that he had a "whole lot to think about" and that the walk would do him good. Grant finally placed his hand on his shoulder and forced Luke to meet his eye.

"You know that Heather's been through a hell of a lot over the past couple of years," Grant said timidly, out there on the porch.

"I know that."

"When we lost Max, it was like..." Grant shook his head ominously. "It was like a meteorite crashing through our family."

"I can understand that." Luke's throat tightened with sorrow.

"That doesn't mean I don't think you and Heather both deserve future happiness," Grant breathed. "Maybe it's just two steps forward, three steps back. That's all."

"And maybe she'll never be ready. And I'll have to respect that, too," Luke returned.

Grant nodded tentatively. "I'm sorry, Luke."

Luke turned on his heel and headed toward the road. But as he walked back toward his place, his hands shoved in his pockets, he came to terms with the only truth he fully knew. He'd hurt Heather. He'd made her feel very small. And if they couldn't be lovers and partners, then he wanted to make sure that they could always be friends.

He had to fix this if only to keep the beautiful friendship they'd once had. He had to do something, and fast.

Chapter Ten

The address Hannah sent her mother wasn't familiar to Angie. Since her drop-out, Angie had thought Hannah remained at the four-bedroom apartment in Logan's Square, together with three other girls she'd met at university. Apparently, Hannah's life had surged forward, morphed and changed, all without any cause to alert her mother. When Angie typed Hannah's new address into her map application, she found that Hannah's new place sat squarely in what Angie would term a "bad neighborhood." It certainly wasn't an area Angie would have walked through by herself.

The drive from Cincinnati to Chicago was meant to take only five hours or so. With the morning traffic outside of Indianapolis, plus a horrific crash on I-65, the drive took Angie nearly seven. Throughout, she gripped the steering wheel of her car with bright white fingers, panicked about what came next.

"Hi, Hannah. I'm adopted and I can't imagine ever giving you up in a million years, not even now that you've refused to talk to me for over six months. It's made me really confused about the nature of my past and where I come from. And it's made me miss you more than life itself."

She practiced the words to the Indiana air as she pressed her foot on the brake and lifted it off again, weaving her way past the accident site.

Felix and Angie had prided themselves on being good, creative, doting parents. During the early days, they'd always been quick to roll around with Hannah on the floor or paint pictures or teach her to learn a new instrument. "Seeing the world through Hannah's eyes is one of the greatest gifts," Felix had said once, and Angie had totally agreed. Throughout this early period of Hannah's life, their jazz music had escalated, becoming something more emotional and heightened. Their audiences had noticed the difference and come out in droves. The Lake City Rollers had been on fire.

Felix and Angie had discussed having more children but had decided that, as musicians, they didn't have so much money to spread around. It was better to give all their love and attention to just one beautiful, perfect creature— Hannah.

"What do you want to be when you grow up?" Angie had cradled a four-year-old Hannah as night had fallen outside their Hyde Park apartment.

"An astronaut," Hannah had cried first. "No. A scientist. No. A musician. No..."

Angie parked her car alongside the snowdrift that toiled in front of a shoddy-looking apartment building. Her heart seized with worry. Was this really where her daughter resided? She grabbed her phone and checked the address again, praying it was someplace else, but no, this was it.

Unfortunately, her daughter hadn't given her the apartment number. Angie dropped her head back on the car seat, feeling defeated. She sipped the cold coffee she'd purchased from a gas station outside of Cincinnati seven hours before. It reeked.

Angie considered texting Hannah again about the apartment number. She was terrified that Hannah had suddenly decided that she didn't want her mother in her life, after all. It wouldn't take a lot for her to figure out who her grandfather's lawyer was. She could easily get the money that way at age thirty, in ten years.

Just when Angie contemplated giving up, one of the ground-floor apartment doors flew open. A broad-shouldered man of approximately six feet, three inches, stormed out of the door, pushing his arms into his coat sleeves as he howled at the person behind him. It was clear from his clothing and his neck tattoo and the way he walked that he was trouble. What's more, it was clear that he wanted to be trouble and nothing more or less. He whipped around to howl back at the woman in the doorway, saying words that Angie would never have repeated—words that Felix would have never said to her.

As the man strutted away, Angie's eyes landed on the woman in the doorway. Her face was sallow, pale, and lifeless. Reddish-brown curls wafted around her shoulders, and she wore a baggy navy sweatshirt and oversized navy sweatpants. Thick black makeup lined her eyes, and her lips were thick and parted slightly, as though she stood there in shock.

This woman in the doorway. This woman was her Hannah.

As Hannah began to close the door, Angie scrambled from her vehicle, nearly slipping on a slab of ice. She then rushed for the door, her heart pounding. How could she translate just how much she'd missed Hannah? Were words ever enough to show how much you loved someone? Or were words just words?

Once outside the door, Angie lifted her knuckles and knocked. There was the pound-pound-pound of Hannah's feet as she rushed back. When she ripped open the door, Angie sensed that Hannah thought she was that guy from before. Hannah was ready for another round of whatever fight they'd just had.

But when Hannah's eyes found her mother's, Hannah froze with her hand on the doorknob. Angie remained on the front stoop, captivated. For hours and hours, throughout the visitation and the funeral of Chester Fitzgerald, Angie had watched the doorway expectantly, waiting for Hannah to suddenly walk through.

But that Hannah was gone now, replaced with this strange version with hollowed-out cheeks. What had happened to her? And who was that man?

"Hannah..." Angie began softly.

Hannah's face crumpled. For a long moment, Angie expected Hannah to rip into her— to demand why she had come, to ask why she didn't respect Hannah's wishes to be left alone. But instead, Hannah suddenly hung forward so that her forehead landed on Angie's shoulder. She shook as sobs escaped her. Motherly instinct brought Angie's arms around her daughter. She held her tightly as her shoulder grew damp with her daughter's tears.

Whatever this pain was, Angie would do her best to take it all away. Whatever had happened in the past would stay in the past. Now, her daughter needed her. And she would do what she could to keep both their heads above water.

Chapter Eleven

Luke had never been on an airplane. He tried to explain this to the woman at the Bangor security airport line as, one by one, she removed his articles and insisted on throwing away one-half of his toiletries. The woman sounded flippant when she said, "You've never flown? Well, that's why the airlines send you the list of what not to pack. It's for this very reason." Luke slid his much-lighter backpack over his shoulder and sauntered away from security like a wounded animal. If he really did see Heather again, he decided not to tell her about this incident. He didn't want her to think he was too green.

Once on the plane, he loosened up a bit. He read a magazine about some newfound culinary arts in the New England area and took notes in his notepad. When the older man beside him took an interest in what he wrote, Luke explained to him in an excited tone about the Acadia Eatery and Nicole's quest to make it one of the most successful restaurants on the east coast.

"I might have to try this place out," the man replied as Luke showed off some photos from the Keating Inn. "I never get over to Bar Harbor. It always looks like heaven on earth."

"It is," Luke assured him. "Breaks my heart to fly away."

"What brings you to New York?" the man asked.

Luke pondered his answer for a long moment. It was heavy on his tongue, yet oddly embarrassing to say aloud.

"I have to go see about a girl," Luke finally said.

"Ah," the man tapped the side of his nose. *"Good Will Hunting?* I haven't seen the movie in years. Fantastic cast." He then grabbed a bag of peanuts from his bag and offered Luke some. "I always get the munchies in the air."

Luke's heart swelled with a mix of embarrassment and excitement. Had he ever done anything this dramatic in his life? All night, he'd tossed and turned in bed, his mind toiling between what was possible to do and what wasn't. He certainly had the money to fly to NYC, and a quick online search found him the address of the stage where Heather would record her interview the following evening. He imagined himself there, poised at the entrance to the stage, a rose in hand. He would catch Heather before she headed onto stage and tell her...

Well? What would he tell her? That he treasured their friendship above all things? That he wanted to love her as best as he could, but that if she didn't want that, he would... Well? What? What would he do if she really, officially rejected his love? He wasn't entirely sure.

The plane ride was swift and terrifying. It was difficult for Luke to comprehend that people did this sort of thing all the time. They latched themselves with seatbelts onto seats that flew thousands of feet into the air. And then, when the plane landed, they acted as though nothing had happened at all.

JFK was a smorgasbord of sounds and smells, a meeting place for people from all over the world going north, south, east, and west. Bug-eyed, Luke ducked out of the airport and hustled for the cab line, where he waited for ten minutes before an available cab driver asked him where he wanted to go.

In the back of the cab, Luke positioned his backpack beneath his arm and listened as the cab driver told him a story about his aunt, whom he seemed to live with, and her insistence that he eat "a full pasta meal" before every work shift. "I'm fully stuffed by the time I get in this cab," the driver told him. "And then all I do is sit! I swear, I've gained fifteen pounds since I started driving. My aunt's happier than ever. She's one of these Italian women who just wants to fatten you up. Ah, but you know. That's what families are all about."

"Yeah," Luke replied in agreement, as though he knew exactly what he meant.

He'd informed the driver to drop him off several blocks north of the place where Heather's interview was supposed to be conducted, as the interview itself was still a few hours away and Luke didn't want to hang out outside the stage and twiddle his thumbs until Heather's arrival.

"You've been to New York before, haven't you?" the driver asked as they got closer to Luke's destination.

"I lived here for a little while."

"I thought so." The driver snapped his fingers. "You have that look about you. Like you understand the way things work around here. Like Anthony Bourdain or someone like that."

"That's pretty good company," Luke replied.

"Hey, you should hear how much my aunt loves Anthony Bourdain," the driver told him. "When he passed away, it devastated all of us."

Three blocks north of the studio, Luke paused outside of a coffee shop and adjusted his backpack across his shoulders. The cost of the cab ride had been more than he'd bargained for, which was probably the first in a long line of things that would remind Luke that he'd been away from New York for far too long.

Luke ducked into the coffee shop to order a bagel and a cup of coffee. It was true what they said about New York bagels: they didn't make them as good anywhere else. A bakery in Bar Harbor tried their darnedest but still came up short.

Luke sat in the corner booth of the coffee shop with his bagel, his cream cheese, and his steaming cup of coffee. As he sat, nibbling the outer edge of his bagel, the clouds above NYC darkened and cast large raindrops upon the sidewalk. Pedestrians sped forward, drawing umbrellas out of their backpacks and purses and casting them overhead. Luke took another bite of his bagel, wondering where Heather was in all this mayhem.

A half-hour later or so, the rain petered out, and Luke found himself on the streets he'd once known. He shoved his hands in his pockets and walked like a ghost through New York City, amazed at the difference just ten or so years made. Not a single shop or bar, or restaurant seemed the same as it was before. There was no commitment to anything in New York, not like in Bar Harbor. There, even the bar he frequented was over fifty years old.

The first thirty or forty minutes of Luke's walk made him introspective and internally morose in ways that surprised him. After nearly an hour, strange thoughts occurred to him about his relationship with Heather. She was about to have a book made into a film, for goodness sakes, while all he did, night and day, was chop carrots, onions, and garlic in a restaurant that would never be his. Why would she stick with him?

By the time five o'clock rolled around, Luke had nearly convinced himself to just head home and give up, that he wasn't worthy of her love. He was again just a few blocks from where Heather was set to record her interview, but already, he felt like a strange and weak man, someone who couldn't understand the city or how the world worked any longer. Perhaps he was better off in his cabin on Frenchman Bay, where he could live out his days alone.

But he had come all that way, hadn't he? He decided to wander over to the studios and just see them, just to know where Heather was. Perhaps he would receive some kind of sign.

When he reached the studios, his stomach tightened with regret. The place was anticlimactic, tiny, and painted a terribly ugly black. Luke wrapped his hands over the top of the fence around the property and made peace with the fact that there was no "sign" to be had here.

But suddenly, he heard his name.

"Luke?"

Luke yanked his head around to find Bella and Kristine hustling toward him. They came from the opposite direction, both carrying little doggy bags of leftover food. Bella flung her arms around him first and placed her head tenderly on his shoulder. His heart calmed for a brief moment. Over the late summer and into the fall, he'd really taken to Kristine and Bella, frequently joking with them and building a sort of friendship. Probably, they weren't so keen about their mother "moving on" from their father. He guessed it would take years for any sort of acceptance surrounding their father's death. Luke was the first to understand that "acceptance" didn't always breed peace.

"What are you doing here?" Kristine asked, her face marred with confusion.

"I um—" Luke palmed the back of his neck nervously.

"You wanted to surprise Mom!" Bella interjected suddenly.

"I don't know about that," Luke replied quickly, even as his cheeks burned bright with shame.

"Oh gosh, but you probably don't have a pass for the show?" Kristine asked.

Luke gaped at her. He hadn't imagined himself this far

through the story. *A pass?* He'd only imagined himself talking to Heather somewhere backstage.

"Maybe I could just talk with your mother before she goes on stage?"

Kristine cackled knowingly. "I don't think so. They already kicked us out a little over an hour ago, which is why we grabbed snacks." She gestured toward the doggy bag.

"Ah. Gotcha," Luke scratched the back of his head as he tried to think of what to do next.

Bella grabbed Luke's wrist, tugging him toward the entrance of the black building as her eyes glistened. When they reached the doorway, both Kristine and Bella flashed their passes at the guard before Bella stated, "This man is family. He arrived too late to receive his pass."

The security guard arched an eyebrow at Luke doubtfully.

"And we're the twin daughters of the main interview today." Kristine reminded him.

The guard turned his gaze back toward the belly of the studio and nodded discretely, as though this was a breach of his contract. Bella tugged Luke the rest of the way into the studio, grinning excitedly. Both twins felt that they'd gotten away with something.

The backstage area was a flurry of activity. Camera workers flew past in a rush; the makeup crew hurried back toward a collection of well-lit mirrors. The talk show host herself, May Wilkerson, breezed past wearing a dark blue power suit, her red hair coiled up into a perfect yet severe bun.

Luke found the back of Heather's perfect head near the makeup mirrors. He felt tugged in her direction. Even his toes twitched in that direction. He needed to drop down before her mirror and place his hands on her knees and tell her just how certain he was about her. He needed to let her know the truth.

"I want to talk to your mother for a moment," Luke told Kristine and Bella, his eyes widening.

"We don't have time," Kristine said. "The interview is set to begin in five minutes. You don't want to freak her out, do you?"

"There's a lot riding on this for Mom," Bella affirmed.

Bella and Kristine led him into the studio audience seating, where two seats had been set aside for Kristine and Bella near the stage. Kristine simply moved one of the "assigned" seat tags down one to allow for Luke to sit between them. "That was easy," she teased.

"Kristine..." Bella sighed.

"What? It's not like anyone else here is as close to Mom as we are," Kristine returned.

The lights began to dim. Luke's heart pumped with adrenaline and fear. He collapsed in the free chair and gripped the end of his knees, watching the far end of the stage intently. What would happen when Heather stepped out on stage and spotted him? Would she think he was insane? Probably. And would she be wrong? Probably not.

Luke had always thought himself to be too good for any sort of romantic involvement. Yet here he was— lost in a flurry of emotion. He'd flown all the way to the city, for goodness sake. He deserved whatever fate awaited him.

Chapter Twelve

The first thing Angie noticed about Hannah's apartment was the smell. The assaulting smell rolled out of the back kitchen and down the hallway, which seemed to be a mixture of rotting food, cigarettes, and bad alcohol. Angie's stomach twisted with pain and sorrow. Hannah's eyes reflected understanding. She knew about the smell. She was aware of the mess, but no longer had the strength to do anything about it. Perhaps it had gone on too long.

"Can I get you a glass of water?" Hannah finally asked.

Angie shook her head. "I don't need anything."

Hannah lifted her shoulder toward her ear and then dropped onto the edge of the couch. Someone had smoked a cigarette recently indoors and left one-half of it in the ashtray on the coffee table. Hurriedly, Hannah whisked the ashtray to the back of the house as Angie sat on the floor on a patch of carpet that seemed clean. When Hannah returned, she apologized for the cigarettes.

"I keep asking him to quit."

Angie breathed a sigh of relief that Hannah wasn't the smoker, at least. She still respected her body enough not to go down that road.

"What is your boyfriend's name?" Angie heard herself ask politely.

"Gary," Hannah replied.

"Gary," Angie repeated it because she couldn't say anything else.

The television on the far wall was the largest and most expensive television that Angie had ever seen. She and Felix had never wanted a television in the house, as it distracted them from making music. Was this why Hannah had opted for such a large screen? Or was this Gary's decision?

Hannah flicked on the television then, perhaps just because the silence between them was deafening. At first, Angie was oddly grateful for the sound, as it drowned out her fears around being alone with her daughter for the first time in many months. But after a moment, the sound was like fingernails on a chalkboard.

Still, Angie didn't want to suggest they turn it down. Perhaps Hannah was so accustomed to the sound that she no longer registered it.

"I was surprised to see that you moved out of Logan's Square," Angie said finally.

"What?" Hannah asked as she couldn't fully hear Angie over the blare of the television.

"I was surprised you left Logan's Square," Angie said again, this time much louder. Her voice sounded strained.

"Oh, yeah." Hannah placed the remote control on the couch and studied the carpet. She didn't add anything else.

"But you must have met Gary since I last..." Angie wanted to say, 'Since I last saw you,' but she held her tongue.

"We met in July, I guess," Hannah told her.

Several pieces of her daughter's puzzle clicked into place. The crazy partying that had led to Hannah's ultimate decision to drop out of university and the feeling that Hannah drifted further and further away into nothingness. Perhaps not all of it could be blamed on the boy. At this moment, however, Angie nearly seethed with rage. Didn't he know how talented she was? Didn't he know how he wasted her life?

"It's good to see you, Mom," Hannah murmured suddenly, speaking more to the carpeting than to Angie.

Angie's heart lifted into her throat. She wasn't sure what she'd expected this day to be— but this was far from her imagination. Her throat tightened as she struggled to find the words to tell her daughter just how much she'd missed her over the past six months.

Angie's phone began to buzz. She dragged out the cell to find FELIX plastered across the front screen. She groaned inwardly and then ignored the call. Hannah's face shifted. She'd noticed the name.

"Have you been in contact with your father at all?" Angie asked softly, already knowing the answer.

Hannah shook her head quickly. Her eyes glittered. "I don't want to talk to him."

This broke Angie's heart all the more. The three of them had once been a perfect team. They hadn't needed anyone else. Now, they seemed like three islands floating at a great distance from one another, with no bridges in between.

The television blared a commercial for a carpet cleaner that might have done wonders in that very apartment. Angie's tongue lifted, as though it had a mind of its own and wanted to tell Hannah what's-what about cleaning.

But Hannah knew her mother much better than Angie realized.

"Just don't, Mom..." Hannah sighed, exasperated.

Angie's hands wrapped around her knees. "What do you mean?"

"Just... I know what you want to say. So just don't, okay?"

"I still don't know what you mean," Angie tried. Why should she be persecuted for something she'd wanted to say but hadn't?

"Come on, Mom. It's written all over your face." Hannah gestured around the apartment, her ring catching the blue light from the television. "You want to tear through this mess. You can't believe I'm dating a smoker. You can't believe I left Logan's Square and those goody-two-shoes girls. You don't even know where to start with all of this because actually, you came all this way to rip into me about how I missed Grandpa's funeral."

Angie's nostrils flared with genuine shock. Her daughter's anger toward her was sharp-edged. Unsure of why or how, Angie rose to the occasion, matching her daughter.

"You know what, Hannah. To be honest with you, I thought that even after all we've been through, after all the ways you've failed yourself, you wouldn't actually miss your Grandpa's funeral. You loved him. You actually loved him! And you didn't even take the time to say goodbye one final time! I just can't understand how the daughter I raised could ever do something like that!"

Hannah blinked back tears. Angie, who hadn't spoken her mind at all over the past few weeks— not since the discovery of her husband's affair nor the death of her father nor the realization that she was adopted— now found a way to cut loose and it felt amazing for once.

"All I ever wanted for you was a decent life, Hannah," Angie continued. "And that's all anyone else in Cincinnati wanted for you, too! When everyone came up to me at the funeral and asked about you, I had to feed them lies. Lies that you're still going to school and that you're doing well. In reality, I hadn't even spoken to you in six months!"

Angie felt her own tears roll down her cheeks as tears fell from Hannah's eyes. Angie had said enough.

"I just couldn't make it! Okay?" Hannah cried suddenly, her eyes widening. "I loved my grandfather, and I missed his funeral, and I'll never get that time back, and I know that. Okay? Can we please just drop it?"

Angie snapped her lips together in surprise. Her finger found the outer edge of the manila folder she'd stolen from the records office in Cincinnati. Maybe this moment of tension was the opportune moment to drop the bomb.

With the manila folder open on the coffee table, Angie brought out the driver's license photocopies alongside the adoption papers that listed her as ANGELA BARRINGTON. Hannah's jaw dropped as she leaned forward to assess everything.

"Mom. What is all this?"

Angie shook her head in disbelief. "I have no idea."

Hannah read and reread the adoption papers as the end of her index finger circled the names ANGELA, CHESTER, and her grandmother, HANNAH.

"You were adopted," Hannah whispered simply as her eyes found Angie's.

"I don't know what to make of it," Angie whispered. "I just can't believe my father never told me."

"And these people are your real parents?" Hannah asked, her voice catching. "This woman... your real mother?" She held Wendy's driver's license photo alongside Angie's face and took in the resemblance. "You could be twins," Hannah added.

"You know how much I loved my mother," Angie said.

"I know. You named me after her," Hannah whispered.

"Yes, but learning about this woman who actually gave birth to me is putting me through the wringer. I don't know where to put my love for my mother now. I don't know how to have any feeling for this stranger who looks just like me."

Hannah nodded simply as her shoulders slanted toward the ground. "When did you discover this?"

"A few days ago," Angie said.

Hannah shook her head ominously.

"What?" Angie demanded.

"I just can't believe you've had to carry this alone," Hannah murmured. "On top of the divorce. On top of losing your jazz band. On top of Grandpa Chester's death."

Against her better judgment, a sob escaped Angie's lips. She clapped her hand over her mouth and dropped her chin to her chest.

"Who told you about the divorce? And the band?" Angie managed to rasp.

Hannah shrugged. "A friend…" She shook her head, stumbling over the words. "A friend takes bass lessons from Autumn and…" She closed her eyes as devastation took hold. "She saw Autumn and Dad together and asked about them. Autumn told her they'd taken the jazz band in a new direction. That he was divorcing his wife."

"You've known all this time…"

Hannah blinked back tears. "It was like hearing a story about someone else's life. Not mine."

"I feel the same way," Angie told her. "Like someone else took the reins on my story and I no longer have any say."

There, in the dramatic mess of Hannah's life, Angie felt herself finally break down. Hannah placed a hand on the top of Angie's back and rubbed at the muscle, which was terribly stiff after the seven-hour drive. Through her tear-streaked vision, Angie spotted Hannah's trumpet case in the corner, on which she and Gary had piled up a number of magazines and newspapers and unpaid bills. Angie's heart seized with the memory of the first time Hannah had ever made her first sound on the trumpet. Felix had been overjoyed.

"We'll figure this out, Mom," Hannah whispered. "I promise you that."

But Angie wasn't sure exactly what she meant. How would Hannah, with her limited experience and her own messed-up life, help Angie figure anything out?

"Thank you, honey," Angie breathed. "That means a lot."

Chapter Thirteen

Hannah and Angie sat in silence for another twenty minutes. Angie's thoughts slowly ate their way from circling terror back into the real world. With the television still booming, Angie found herself focusing on the commercials as they popped in and out, selling tickets to Six Flags theme park, five-dollar foot-longs, and half-price tire changes if you came in before three on a weekday. The characters in the commercial seemed overly bright and confident to Angie. Weren't they just unemployed actors? Why were they so good at faking it?

Throughout, Hannah continued to study the photographs of her "real" grandparents, Wendy and Glenn Barrington. Finally, she lifted Glenn's photo to the light and said, "He really was handsome, wasn't he?"

Angie made a strange sound in her throat.

"I just can't imagine what happened," Hannah breathed. "They had you for a year and a half before they..." Hannah stumbled, not knowing the correct terminology.

Angie shrugged. "Having a child that age is tough. I get it."

Hannah's face grew shadowed.

Angie hurriedly added, "Not that I would have ever given you up. Not in a million years. It didn't even occur to me once." She sounded terribly fierce, almost angry. Maybe she was angry. Why had her parents wanted to give her up? Hadn't she been just as helpless as any other baby? She'd seen photographs from back then, her mother Hannah wrapping her up in a blanket as they read out on the front porch overlooking downtown Cincinnati. The parents who'd created her hadn't thought she was enough. Perhaps that was her curse.

A talk show began on the large television. The host, known colloquially as "May," clacked out onto the screen in high heels and a power suit. Her hair seemed to evade gravity. She greeted the gathered crowd with a bright, "Isn't this a beautiful day?" before she stomped the rest of the way to the chair center-stage and grinned at the camera. Angie had never seen this talk show before, but she had it on her radar. Everyone did. It was just a show that came on every day at five-thirty, come sun or rain. You could count on it.

"Today, we have a very exciting show planned for you all," May began. "You all know how passionate I am about reading, especially when it comes to making young adults excited about it. There's nothing I love more than when my daughter and I sit out on the balcony with our books and a big pitcher of lemonade. Hours and hours float away like that. Truly treasured memories."

The crowd whooped and hollered. Angie gave a sidelong glance to Hannah, who didn't return it. Hannah and Angie had spent similar afternoons throughout Hannah's youth, during which they'd read one book after another side-by-side. Angie would have given up a lot to return to those moments.

"My daughter first introduced me to our guest," May continued. "She became obsessed with her fantasy series, which has just been optioned to be made into a movie. Her name is Heather Harvey Talbot— and she's just about as sweet as can be. Heather! Come on out to the stage!"

The crowd roared as the striking Heather Harvey Talbot stepped out onto the stage. She looked confident, her shoulders back and her chin high. Her ocean-blue eyes glittered knowingly, showing just the slightest hint of nerves.

"Did you ever read any of her books?" Angie asked Hannah.

Hannah, who'd again burrowed herself into the adoption papers, lifted her eyes back to the screen just as they flashed an image of Heather's fantasy book collection.

"Yeah, actually. When I was fourteen or fifteen, I think," Hannah replied. "Before they got really big." To Angie, Hannah had been fourteen or fifteen approximately five minutes ago. Where had the time gone?

"They're going to make it into a movie," Angie recited.

Hannah muttered a soft yet disinterested, "Wow."

Angie collected herself on the couch alongside Hannah, deciding that she no longer wanted to sit on the carpet. On-screen, May began to ask Heather a series of questions about her upcoming book and her movie debut.

"What did you say when you first learned that your books were being optioned for the screen?" May asked.

Heather puffed out her cheeks adorably. "Gosh, I don't know. At first, I actually said I didn't want that. You know? Because these stories had only existed in my head for over a decade, and I wasn't sure I wanted to give creative control to anyone else."

"I could understand that," May replied. "What made you change your mind?"

"My daughters, I suppose," Heather said. "Kristine and Bella. They're my dream girls. They told me that this was a once-in-a-lifetime opportunity. That I would be silly to pass it up."

The camera panned toward the audience, where two beautiful twenty-something women sat on either side of a handsome man, presumably Heather's husband. The man smiled nervously, knowing the camera was on him. He was not entirely happy about it.

"I just can't get it through my head," Hannah breathed. "That Grandpa never even told Grandma Janice about adopting you. You would have thought he'd at least have mentioned it. Why would he want to keep a secret like that for so long?"

Angie shrugged. "I don't know. It's not like he was ever averse to making me feel like an alien in my own life. This seems like a perfect tool in his arsenal."

Hannah grumbled inwardly.

"I know. Grandpa was never like that toward you. And I'm so grateful for that," Angie added. "But he was never that nice to me. I guess he just never bonded with the little girl he picked up from the orphanage. Imagine that."

"He still raised you," Hannah tried.

"Yeah? Well, I raised you," Angie said angrily. "And you haven't answered my calls in six months."

This silenced Hannah for a number of minutes. Angie immediately regretted her words yet didn't have the strength to take them back. She focused on the writer who was on the talk show, who now spoke about how she would work alongside the screenwriters who would turn her book into a working movie script.

"Now, I hope you don't mind that I bring this up, but you mentioned previously that these past couple of years have been very difficult for you," May, the talk show host, continued.

Heather's eyes grew shadowed. It seemed clear that she didn't want to discuss whatever this was. "Yes. We, um. We lost my husband in a terrible accident about a year and a half ago."

Angie shrieked at the screen. "Why did you have to make her talk about that?"

Hannah guffawed. "Seriously? She was so happy before. Now she looks like she's about to burst into tears."

"It's been a terrible road," Heather continued as the camera panned in closer to her ocean-blue eyes. "But last year, my sisters and I started to work together at the inn our father left us in Bar Harbor, Maine."

"Bar Harbor. It's such a magical place," May cooed.

"It really is," Heather admitted. "I was born there but never really spent much time until now. For us Harvey girls, it was cursed for a number of years."

"But the curse is broken?" May asked.

"You could say that." Heather's face shifted slightly. She seemed lost in thought, gazing at something off-camera. Her lips parted in surprise as she suddenly said, "Oh! Gosh. Hi."

The camera jumped back to get a bigger picture of the audience, Heather, and the talk show host.

"You look surprised," May noted just then. "Who do you see in the audience?"

Heather paused for a long time, collecting herself. "Someone surprised me today." A secret smile spread from ear to ear.

The camera followed her line of sight back toward the twins. The handsome man who sat between them blushed even more than he had previously. His cheeks were ruby red. With the camera on him, he lifted a hand to greet Heather timidly. To that, Heather laughed gently.

"Who is that man?" May asked Heather.

"Oh gosh. He's... he's one of the most important people in my life," Heather replied. "I couldn't have imagined the past six months without him. He saved me in numerous ways. And his forgiveness for my silliness seems never-ending."

The audience roared at the mention of "forgiveness."

Hannah scoffed again and said, "They really lean into cheesiness territory when it comes to these talk shows, don't they?"

"Why don't we have your friend come up here and introduce himself?" May, the talk show host suggested, seeing the way the audience took to him immediately.

"Luke? Will you come up?" Heather asked gently.

The crowd roared again as Luke stood and jumped up the steps to join the woman center-stage. Angie had been wrong. He wasn't Heather's husband. He was someone new in her life.

Did this kind of thing give Angie hope for her future? That you could experience tremendous loss and still have so much to gain?

Maybe not, she thought now. After all, she and Heather Harvey Talbot were very different creatures in the world. Heather seemed to always get what she wanted. Angie, not so much.

"Good to see you, Luke," May, the talk show host, began brightly. A staff member hustled out from backstage to attach a small microphone to Luke's button-down shirt.

"Good to be here," Luke countered. He glanced toward Heather, his smile giddy. Clearly, he loved her.

"Heather says that you've been a source of comfort and joy over the previous six months of her life," May continued. "Do you have anything to add to that?"

Luke blushed again and turned his eyes toward Heather. "I met Heather during a very difficult time of her life. On top of her personal tragedy, she learned something about her past—something that aligned with my past in tremendous ways."

"Yes," Heather interjected. "I'm not ashamed to say it. I learned that the two people I'd always thought to be my birth parents weren't my birth parents at all."

A hush ran over the crowd. Angie's jaw dropped with recognition.

"What did she just say?" Hannah hissed.

Luke picked up where Heather dropped off. "I was raised in foster care in Ohio. I was tossed around from orphanage to foster home. I never really felt like I belonged anywhere."

"He helped me discover the truth of my birth parents. He helped me move on from that wound and find new ground. He just got what I was going through. He understood the displacement I felt," Heather breathed as she reached across the chair and took Luke's hand.

"Wow. What are the odds?" Angie whispered. She lifted her sleeve to the corner of her eye to wipe a tear away. "And look at them. They love each other so much."

Beside Angie, Hannah remained very quiet. The camera continued to pan closer and closer to Heather and Luke's faces, where they shared a quiet moment of joy. Suddenly, Hannah grabbed the remote control and paused the image where it was.

"Hey!" Angie cried, embarrassed that she'd gotten so invested in the story.

But suddenly, Hannah grabbed the old driver's license photocopy of Glenn Barrington and lifted it between Angie and the television before them. Her hand shook with fear.

The man in the old photocopy and the man on screen were nearly identical.

Angie's lips parted with surprise. Laughter erupted through her. "No. You can't be serious," she gasped.

But Hannah's eyes bugged out of her head. "Look at them, Mom. Look at their eyes. At their hair. At the cut of their chin."

Angie's heart thudded wildly in her chest. It was totally outside the bounds of reason. It didn't make any sense.

Hannah leaped up from the couch, quicker than she'd moved all day, and then placed the photocopy directly on the TV screen next to Luke's face.

"Tell me these people aren't related," Hannah said.

Angie had no words. With a quivering hand, she reached

for the remote control and rewound the talk show about thirty seconds back. She watched, captivated until Luke repeated the words:

"I was raised in foster care in Ohio."

"See?" Hannah cried. "Ohio!"

Angie placed her hands on her cheeks and fell back into the stained cushions of her daughter's couch. This was impossible, wasn't it? It didn't make any sense.

Chapter Fourteen

New York City, New York

"And that's a wrap!" The director of May's talk show finished out the half-hour as the crowd roared with applause. May's eyes were dewy and grateful. She dropped forward and first squeezed Luke's hand, then Heather's.

"Thank you for sharing your stories today," May beamed sweetly. "My audience eats up a good love story."

Luke's heart swelled as he glanced in Heather's direction. He half-expected Heather to insist they were "just friends." Maybe by now, the jig was up. She had to admit the truth of their dynamic. She had to admit that when she'd spotted him in the audience, far and away from their Bar Harbor home, she'd realized the depths of her feelings. Or at least, she'd realized they were in too deep to turn back now.

Luke and Heather headed backstage, where their microphones were removed. Heather continued to beam as though her smile was taken directly from the sun. Kristine and Bella threw their arms around their mother and performed little shrieks of, "You looked so good up there!" and, "My mother's book is about to become a major movie!" Luke wasn't sure where to put his hands. On his waist? Crossed over his chest?

"I can't believe she pulled you up on stage!" Bella remarked to Luke as she drew a strand of hair behind her ear.

"I wasn't fully ready for that either," Luke admitted.

"But you did amazing," Kristine said. "May had a total crush on you after two seconds."

"I know. I was jealous," Heather teased.

Kristine, Bella, Luke, and Heather decided to cross the busy intersection nearby to grab some coffees and slices of cake to share at a tiny coffee shop. Luke was surprised and pleased at how comfortable he felt in their midst. He teased Kristine and kept up with Bella's sarcasm and found his hand brushing Heather's knee, which made her smile. He and Heather shared a slice of carrot cake with cream cheese frosting, and Heather's eyes closed at the luxurious flavor as she licked icing from the tongs of her fork.

"Nicole refuses to make anything like this these days," Heather said. "It always has to be the most intricate and difficult cake recipe. Something as simple as carrot cake doesn't cut it for her anymore."

"She's gotten insanely good, though," Kristine said warmly.

"She has," Heather agreed. "I just wouldn't mind the occasional chocolate chip cookie."

"You know, you're talking to a mediocre cook who can whip up some of the best chocolate chip cookies in the land..." Luke quipped, pounding his chest jokingly.

"That's right," Heather added as she pointed her fork toward him. "You're not mediocre. But you're definitely not trying to prove anything, like my sister."

"That's right. I'll make you junk food any time you like it," Luke said. "And I'll make it better than anyone else."

"It's a deal," Heather returned, her eyes alight.

Kristine and Bella exchanged glances. To Luke, and perhaps to everyone else, this conversation seemed to be about something else. Kristine lifted a large morsel of cake to her lips and chewed quickly. Bella grabbed her purse from beneath the table.

"We have to get going," Kristine announced.

"Where are you two off to?" Heather asked.

"We have a thing," Bella said flippantly.

"Yeah. A social function," Kristine affirmed.

"Since when do you two call things 'social functions'?" Heather asked with a laugh.

"Since we, um..." Kristine began.

"Since we grew up, Mom," Bella said as she lifted up to place a kiss on her mother's cheek. "We'll see you tomorrow?"

"Okay," Heather said gently. "Love you. Thanks for taking me to my big gig today."

"I'm sure it'll be the first of many." Bella wrapped her coat around her shoulders and headed for the door with Kristine hot on her heels.

With the twins out on the chilly streets of Manhattan once more, Heather and Luke fell into a comfortable silence. Heather took another bite of carrot cake as Luke padded the tops of his thighs.

"I think they left us on purpose, don't you?" Heather asked finally, her eyes glittering mischievously.

"I have to think they're always up to something," Luke affirmed. "They're your daughters, after all."

Heather had a small strip of icing on her bottom lip. Luke ached to kiss it off. They hadn't shared a kiss in what seemed like decades. But he didn't want to appear too eager. He'd come this far, from Bar Harbor to New York, and still, she hadn't resisted him. He didn't want to blow it and scare her off.

"What do you say we walk uptown?" Heather suggested

softly. She reached for a napkin and smeared the icing from her lip self-consciously. "I could have a cocktail somewhere dark and secluded. So we could really, you know. Talk."

Luke's heart pumped loudly. He wanted to pinch himself.

"That sounds nice," Luke breathed. "Really nice."

Moments later, Heather and Luke wound their way northbound along the chaotic Manhattan streets. Luke's hand hovered just a few inches from Heather's. He itched to take her small hand in his.

They didn't say a single word to one another for ten blocks. Heather then mentioned that there was a great cocktail bar not far from there. "Kristine and Bella always show me the best spots in town," she told him. "They keep me young."

The cocktail bar was reminiscent of a cocktail bar from the roaring twenties, with flapper girls as waitresses and a man in a top hat behind the bar.

"It's wild that we still celebrate the 1920s like this, isn't it?" Heather said softly as they sat in a corner booth. "It's the twenties all over again."

"I wonder if they'll be celebrating the 2020s in one hundred years," Luke said.

Heather laughed. "I doubt it, although I don't know. We can never feel the magic of our own time, can we?"

"I don't know," Luke joked. "I was pretty sure it couldn't get more magical than the eighties."

"You were just a kid," Heather pointed out.

"I know," Luke affirmed. "But all those hairstyles? The brightly colored clothing? There was nothing normal about it."

Heather shook with laughter. "I think you're right about that."

They ordered two cocktails— a Boulevardier and something called a Grasshopper. The waitress arrived back with two beautiful cocktail glasses and a little bowl of peanuts.

"Are these peanuts also from the twenties?" Luke joked.

"Yes. Antique peanuts," Heather joined in. "Nothing better."

Again, they fell back into silence and studied one another. Luke's throat was parched. He sipped the cocktail to coat it.

"I was so worried that you never wanted to see me again," Luke finally admitted what weighed heavily on his heart.

Heather's eyes widened. "I thought the same about you."

"Heather..." Luke shook his head tentatively. "You know how I feel about you."

This shut Heather up for nearly thirty seconds. She sipped her drink; as her eyes glowed with tears she refused to let fall.

"Why did you do it, Heather?" Luke breathed then. His tone wasn't accusatory. It was soft, loving. "You knew I wanted to tell you how I felt that night."

Heather closed her eyes. She placed her hands on her cheeks and seemed to focus on her breathing.

"I still feel confused. I still feel like such a fool sometimes, Luke," Heather whispered. "Sometimes, I still wake up and think that Max is alive and well. I think we're still in Portland— that the girls are preparing for their piano recitals or headed to soccer practice or studying for their SATs. And then I have to relive the nightmare of what happened. I have to remember that Max is dead, that my mother wasn't really my mother. That my mother was a cruel and calculating woman who used the man I thought was my father for her own capitalistic gain."

Heather heaved a sigh. Luke wanted to reach out and take her hand, but he held himself back.

"And then I have to remember how I've treated you," Heather whispered. "We had such an immediate connection last year. When I looked at you, I recognized a kindred spirit. You were someone who could sit beside me during my darkest hour and know exactly what to say— or when not to speak. I found myself falling for you. And it felt like such a betrayal of my old life. After that, I feel that I yanked you around. I was so into you one moment and then willing to weasel out of your arms the next. It was cruel, Luke. Especially after everything you've been through."

Luke's heart banged. He hadn't imagined such an elaborate apology.

"The fact is, Luke, I do care for you," Heather whispered. She finally forced herself to lift her eyes to his. "I want to be something to you. I want to be loved by you, and I want to love you in return."

Luke's voice crackled as he spoke. "But you can't?"

"I didn't think I could," Heather whispered. "But every moment since I left your place a few nights ago, I've ached with regret. I know that the only thing worse than betraying my former self is betraying my current and future self. This version of me needs happiness, just as much as the past version of me needed happiness. And Luke, May the talk show host saw it clear as day. We're in love with each other. It's time that I allow myself to admit it. It's time that I live in the here-and-now."

Luke nearly toppled the table over after that. He embraced her, pulling her against him, and kissed her frantically like he would never see her again. Her arms wrapped tightly around his broad shoulders, trying to hold onto all of him at once.

"I love you, Heather," Luke whispered, his eyes clenched. "I love you. And I want to protect you. To help you experience joy and happiness, all the days of your life."

Heather shook tenderly against him. "I love you, Luke. I'm so glad we found one another. And I'm so glad that I can finally face my feelings and uphold them for what they are. I'm sorry it took me so long."

* * *

The following morning, Luke awoke beneath white satin sheets in the hotel room Heather's agent had booked for her on the Upper West Side. Memories of the night before flicked around his mind. He made a mental note to make them "permanent" memories, "never to be lost." He wanted to keep them forever.

Heather sat cross-legged in a robe at the far end of the bed. Her skin glowed beautifully with the light that streamed in from the window. The hotel room was located on the twenty-first floor, far above the chaos of traffic. It was like their own little world.

"How did you sleep?" Heather whispered as she placed a hand across his ankle gently.

"It was the best sleep I've had in ages," Luke told her.

"Me too."

They locked eyes for a long, tender moment. Heather drew herself closer to him. He took in the beautiful delicateness of her unique smell, something that seemed perfectly in-tune with his body. "Sometimes, you can't get past someone's smell," a buddy had told him once as they'd discussed dating. "She could be the most beautiful woman in the world, but if she doesn't smell right to you... It wasn't meant to be."

"I've thought about it, Heather," Luke whispered as he drew his fingers through her dark curls.

"Thought about what?"

"About living in truth with you," Luke answered. "About facing the truth. I'm facing how much I love you. I'm facing that I want to build a life with you. And I'm so grateful you want to do that with me, too."

Heather's ocean-blue eyes widened with hope.

"But on top of that, I think I do want to track down my birth parents," Luke breathed.

Heather arched an eyebrow. "Are you sure, Luke? I don't want you to feel pressured to do anything you don't want to do."

"Why wouldn't I want to know the truth? Why wouldn't I want to know where I came from, especially now that I found you?"

Heather's lips parted in surprise. Luke tipped himself forward and took both of her hands gently.

"What if we called the Ohio office this morning? Get it out of the way," Luke whispered. "Just bite the bullet and then go out and have a beautiful breakfast to celebrate."

"Are you sure about this, Luke?"

"I'm pretty sure about everything today," Luke assured her, his grin widening. "With you by my side, of course."

Heather searched through her online documents to find the phone number for the records office in Cincinnati. The phone rang just twice before a woman answered.

"Hi, there. You've reached the downtown Cincinnati records office. How may I help you?"

Heather explained that she'd spoken with the woman about a week before about finding the adoption paperwork for a baby who'd been dropped off at an orphanage nearly forty-four years before. Through the speaker, the woman said, "I remember you, Heather. Of course. I'll head back and find the documents we discussed right now. Give me a minute?"

Luke waited with bated breath. Heather slipped her fingers through his and gave him a tentative smile.

"She shouldn't be long," Heather told him.

A few minutes later, the woman's voice rang through the speakerphone once again, this time sharper and lighter than before. "Hi! I have um, rather strange news."

Heather's face fell. "What's that?"

"It's just that the files we discussed last week. They appear to have been... misplaced."

"Misplaced?" Heather repeated.

"Heather. It's okay," Luke said immediately, as relief fell over him.

"That's ridiculous," Heather interjected.

"I'm terribly sorry, Mrs. Talbot," the woman said. "I can give you a call when they turn up. I'll tear this office up over the next few hours looking."

"Do call me," Heather said firmly.

"Heather..." Luke warned.

"What?" Heather mouthed toward Luke.

"It isn't a big deal," Luke told her again.

"It is! It is a big deal!" Heather returned, her eyes widening.

"I know it's a big deal," the woman on the speakerphone said. "And I'll give you a call first thing when they turn up. Okay?"

"Okay. Thank you," Luke called toward the phone to allow the woman to hear. He then took the phone from Heather's hand and pressed END.

Heather gaped at him, flabbergasted. "I'm sorry," she whispered. "I thought it would be easy. I thought we could figure everything out together."

Luke drew closer to her on the bed and wrapped his arms around her. "We are figuring everything out together," he told her. "All that was in the past. There's no figuring that out. It's like reading about old characters in some fictional book anyway. The only life I need to worry about is the one I have right here with me. Okay?"

Heather nodded. "I just hope I didn't get your hopes up."

"I'm just relieved that we can go get breakfast now," Luke joked. "I'm starving."

"Why didn't you say something?" Heather laughed.

"Heather, I'm always starving," Luke told her. "Society just forces me to eat only three meals per day."

"That's awful," Heather returned, her voice turning sultry and flirtatious.

Luke kissed her cheek, the tip of her nose, and the beautiful butterfly of her lips. They fell into one another again, there upon the heaven-like white sheets. Luke shoved away all thoughts of disappointment as they curled themselves around one another. This was all the family he needed.

Chapter Fifteen

The queen-sized bed in Marie Collin's guest bedroom sat gleaming beneath a near-perfect morning sunbeam. Angie stood in the doorway in her night-gown, a mug of coffee in hand, as her daughter slept on, her long locks strewn across both pillows. Angie had hardly slept a wink the night before. So often, she'd whipped herself around to check that Hannah remained in bed with her. It hadn't been a dream. She had her girl back.

It had been less of a struggle than Angie had suspected, asking Hannah to return to Marie's with her. Apparently, Gary often returned to their apartment late in the night, which disrupted Hannah's sleep and irritated her next-day plans. With the reeking dishes still in the sink and the couch filled with cigarette burns, it wasn't like the apartment made a case for Hannah to stay there alone. Hannah had packed a small yellow backpack and crawled into the front seat of Angie's car. By the time the clock struck eight forty-five that night, Hannah was passed out asleep in Angie's bed.

The potential of this whole other family and this brother

they'd seen on television both thrilled and terrified Angie. Over dinner the night before, Hannah had pestered Angie to go over more of the documents in the file, to dig deeper. Angie hadn't been ready. She'd wanted to ask her daughter questions about her own life— about whether or not she would ever consider leaving Gary for good and go back to university to study. But she didn't want to push too hard on the situation and watch it shatter.

Marie was off for the morning, running a series of errands outside of the city. This left the kitchen fresh and clean for Angie and Hannah when, several minutes later, they walked back in to brew a fresh pot of coffee and order a selection of baked goods from the local bakery.

"If there's anything I know for sure," Hannah told her as she poured coffee grounds into the filter, "it's that family secrets go well with several rounds of sugary baked goods."

"Wiser words have never been spoken," Angie said.

Fifteen minutes later, a teenager delivered the baked goods. Angie tore open the brown paper sack and splayed out the selection on a large pink plate. Donuts stuffed with cream; everything bagels with cream cheese; croissants stuffed with pistachio cream. "We've got the entire cream family taken care of," Hannah joked.

With the baked goods assembled, Angie again opened the files for Glenn and Wendy Barrington. She sipped her mug of coffee while Angie, who had opted for tea, sifted through the first few pages.

"Let's divide and conquer," Hannah suggested. "I'll take the first half of the stack if you take the second."

"What are we looking for, exactly?" Angie asked.

"Anything," Hannah replied. "Don't you want to know everything?"

This seemed like a good point. Angie hunkered down, nibbling at a bagel slathered with cream cheese, carefully reading over the medical records and old signed paperwork from over forty years ago. After a while, her eyes glazed over at the randomness of some of the stuff she read. She learned that her father had a root canal at the age of twenty-three and that her mother suffered two miscarriages prior to her birth. Angie, who'd never suffered a miscarriage herself, felt her heart pang with sorrow. Yes, at one point, this woman had given up her daughter to an orphanage. But in the same breath, it was impossible for Angie to completely understand the woman's story from only some papers in a yellow envelope. Why did people do the things they did? Why did people hurt people? Angie knew the answer better than most: it was because they, themselves, had been hurt.

"Mom! Look at this." Hannah grabbed some medical records from her stack and placed a firm index finger toward the center. The record had been filled out by Wendy Barrington herself, perhaps prior to a doctor's visit. It was remarkable, first of all, to see the curve of her handwriting, which seemed almost perfect.

One of the questions on the record was:

Have you ever given birth? If so, when.

And Wendy had written the following:

MARCH 22, 1974 - LEO BARRINGTON

NOVEMBER 12, 1976 - ANGELA BARRINGTON

FEBRUARY 16, 1978 - LUKE BARRINGTON

Angie's jaw dropped. She reread the names and the dates once more, suddenly terrified. When her eyes found Hannah's, Hannah took a massive, stress-induced bite of croissant.

"It looks like you have some siblings," Hannah finally said.

"Do you remember what the guy's name was on the talk show?" Angie whispered.

Hannah shook her head. "Did they even say it?"

"I can't remember. I was in shock."

"Let me see." Hannah stood up and collected Angie's

laptop from her backpack. She then sat back down and opened it, placing her fingers tentatively on the keys.

"Are you just going to search for their names?" Angie breathed.

"I'm not sure that would do much for us," Hannah told her. "You don't have their last name anymore…"

"Yes, but maybe they didn't give up the boys for adoption," Angie pointed out, her throat tightening. "Maybe they're still called Barrington."

Hannah shrugged and typed out the names— first LEO BARRINGTON, and then LUKE BARRINGTON. There were a number of results for both names, none of which seemed entirely hopeful. Hannah clicked through a few Ohio-based Luke Barringtons where they discovered a Luke who owned a lumberyard west of Cleveland and another Luke who raised money to make his indie movie. The indie movie Luke seemed entirely too young, and the lumberyard Luke was incredibly large, with bright blonde hair. He had nothing in common with Angie's appearance.

"It's insane to even try to find that guy from the talk show, right?" Angie said softly, her nose scrunched up.

"I don't know. It's all kind of crazy, isn't it?" Hannah tried.

"They said something about Bar Harbor. On the show," Angie said hurriedly. "And the writer's name…"

"Heather Harvey Talbot," Hannah blurted out as she hurriedly typed the name into the search engine, alongside, "Bar Harbor family inn."

"Right. She ran some kind of inn with her sisters…" Angie said.

"Wow, there are a lot of articles about the 'Harvey Sisters,'" Hannah said, impressed. "Looks like one of them is the head chef at the… Keating Inn?" Hannah clicked through to find the website for the Keating Inn, which introduced visitors from far and wide to the glorious world of the Keating Inn and Acadia

Eatery, located on the rocky coastline of Maine. Hannah headed for the "Staff" section, where they found photographs of each of the Keating sisters— Nicole, Casey, and Heather, alongside a younger woman named Abby and a very familiar-looking man named—

"Luke!" Hannah and Angie said it in unison.

"That's him, all right," Angie affirmed. "Gosh, look at him." Angie grabbed the old photo of her real father and placed it alongside the photograph of Luke on-screen.

"It's uncanny, Mom," Hannah breathed.

"If he's my 'real' little brother, then why in the heck is he all the way in Maine?" Angie demanded.

"People move," Hannah pointed out. "You did."

"To Chicago. Barely even two states over," Angie corrected.

"Yes, but..." Hannah lifted her shoulder reluctantly.

"What?"

"It sounded like Luke didn't have anyone raise him at all," Hannah replied softly. "He said he was tossed around from foster family to foster family."

"What's your point?" Angie asked.

"It just sounds like he had a whole lot more to run from than you," Hannah explained. "I know your relationship with Grandpa wasn't super cozy or anything. But at least he..."

"I know," Angie whispered, her heart bruised. "He cared for me."

Just then, the kitchen door creaked open to reveal Marie Collins, whose jaw dropped at the sight of Hannah. "Is that my darling Hannah girl?" she cried with excitement as she headed for Hannah, her arms outstretched. Angie had already cried night after night about her belief that she and Hannah would never mend their relationship. All Marie had been able to say was, *'She'll find her way back to you— somehow.'*

"What's all this?" Marie asked about the documents.

Hurriedly, Angie piled them all together and said, "Oh, you know. We wanted to get a head start on... taxes."

"Taxes?" Marie cocked her head. "Right, well. Nice work on that. I wish I was that organized." She then found Angie's eyes and said, "Ang, do you mind if I talk to you for a sec?"

Angie followed Marie into Marie's bedroom, where Marie shut the door and clasped her hands near her chest. Her chin wiggled as she said, "First of all, Ang... I'm just so sorry for your loss. Really."

"Thank you."

"Did you and Hannah mend things down in Ohio?"

"Something like that," Angie said, not wanting to get into it. "It'll be a long road."

"I'm sure," Marie returned. She then pressed her lips together before adding, "Listen. I hate to do this. But you know my sister? The journalist? She's coming to Chicago to work on a story for the next couple of months, and I told her that she could have the guest room."

"Oh..." Angie furrowed her brow.

"I'm so sorry. You'd been in Ohio for so long, and I was thinking, well, if nobody is really using the spare room... Gosh, I should have just asked you before I..."

"No, no. Don't worry about it. She's your sister," Angie assured her.

"You'll figure something out?" Marie asked.

"Sure," Angie said. "When will she be here?"

"In three days... It's too soon, isn't it? You can sleep in my bed for a few nights until you figure something out."

"Seriously, Marie. You've already done so much for me. It's time for me to move on," Angie told her.

Back in the hallway, Angie fell back against the soft shadows and considered what to do next. She could, for example, tell Felix that she and Hannah needed the apartment for a few months until they decided where to go next. After all, it was just as much Hannah and Angie's place as it was Felix's. But something about asking him to leave turned her stomach. Probably, that meant he would just move in with Autumn instead.

There was another issue at hand. Probably, she and Hannah were now in the "honeymoon" phase of their mother-daughter relationship. Would Hannah soon ask to return to her apartment with Gary? Would she want "out," especially now that Angie needed to vacate Marie's residence?

Angie burned with fear and despair. Slowly, she returned to the kitchen area, where Hannah nibbled her way through one-half of a bagel and again read over the medical document that listed LEO and LUKE as Angie's potential siblings.

From the doorway, Angie found her voice.

"I have an idea."

Hannah lifted her chin and stopped chewing. "What is it?"

"I think we should drive there," Angie suggested, biting her bottom lip.

Hannah arched an eyebrow. "Where?"

"Bar Harbor."

"Oh my gosh." Hannah's eyes widened. "To confront Luke about what we've learned?"

Angie shrugged. "On TV, he didn't talk like he had any idea where he came from."

Hannah pondered this. "Do you think he even wants to know?"

"I don't know," Angie answered truthfully. "But I'd like to see him up close. I'd like to shake his hand."

"Do you think you'll be able to tell if he's your brother?" Hannah asked.

"I have no idea," Angie murmured. "I've wanted siblings my whole life. I was really lonely as a kid, waiting around for something to happen, especially after my mother died."

Hannah dropped her gaze to the papers across the table.

Silence fell between them. Angie prayed Hannah wouldn't mention Gary in all of this. She prayed that they could be free of the men who'd held them back all this time.

Hannah placed her hands flat on the table and shrugged. "You know what? What the heck."

The corners of Angie's lips twitched toward a smile. "You want to go with me?"

Hannah nodded, her eyes alight. "There's nothing else I'd rather do."

Chapter Sixteen

Over the span of the next three hours, Hannah charted a course from Chicago to Bar Harbor, Maine. "It should take about nineteen hours," she explained as she showed her mother the map. "I figure we should break it up over three days since we have no time constraints. Just us and the open road."

"Nice work, Thelma," Angie teased, pulling her daughter in for a kiss on her forehead.

"That'll get us there early February, just a couple of weeks before your brother's real birthday," Hannah stated, pointing again to the document Wendy Barrington had filled out forty-plus years ago.

"It's overwhelming," Angie admitted, scrunching her nose.

"Remember. If it gets to be too much, we can just jump in the car and go someplace else," Hannah told her, keeping her voice light. She then paused and dropped her pen back to the table. "Which reminds me of something. Something I have to do."

"What's exactly is that?"

"I was just wondering if, maybe, after we pack up, we can head over to my apartment," Hannah continued. "I just want to pick up some stuff. Before we, you know, leave the state for an undetermined number of days."

"Of course," Angie murmured. "We can do whatever you like before we leave."

It was decided that they stick around Chicago that evening and head out of the city the following morning. Angie was jumpy and nervous but inarticulate, saying foolish things that made Hannah laugh, like, "What do you think he'll want to know about me? I'm basically a mess!" Hannah just returned with, "Mom, he's going to love you. Everyone does." Angie wanted to protest this. She wanted to point to Felix, first of all, and his decision to end their marriage. Thus far, she and Hannah hadn't spoken about the divorce much at all. Probably, that conversation awaited them on the nineteen-hour drive.

The following morning, Angie packed a duffel bag as Hannah stuffed the rest of her things into a backpack. They then drove, wordless, back toward Hannah's small apartment building. Angie sensed that Hannah didn't want to speak about what would happen next. She could practically feel the terrifying thoughts that circled round and round her skull.

Angie parked directly in front of Hannah's ground floor apartment and made eye contact with her daughter.

"Do you want me to go in with you?"

"No," Hannah told her firmly. "I won't be long."

But only a few moments after Hannah disappeared inside, there came the sound of violent yelling. There was a deep and horrible voice of a man echoing out from the apartment. The voice ripped through the air and made the rearview mirror of Angie's car quiver. Hannah's screams came after that. Angie grabbed the steering wheel so tightly that her fingers turned white.

How had Hannah involved herself with someone like this?

Had Angie and Felix made her think that this was the sort of life she deserved?

When Gary's yelling started up again, Angie couldn't take it any longer. She leaped from the car and rushed for the door, prepared to do whatever it took to stand up for her girl. But just before she reached the front door, Hannah's voice interjected.

"Don't you dare contact me, Gary! I'm out of here. Do you understand?"

"Baby, don't..." Gary's volatile voice grew weak.

The front door burst open to reveal Hannah with tear-soaked cheeks and a large duffel bag stuffed with clothes and unzipped at the top. Hannah slammed the door in Gary's face and then whipped past her mother, headed for the car. Angie's legs nearly gave out from under her. She returned to the driver's seat, then turned the engine on, just as Gary burst out of the door and began to scream at them. Pleading hadn't done anything for him. He'd returned to his favorite tactic.

"GET BACK HERE, HANNAH!" He then added a series of expletives, each of which could have pushed Angie to tears. She was grateful to hold them in.

Angie drove quickly, weaving the car through the city and heading onto the I-90. Her fingers remained stiff over the steering wheel. She also had to bite down on her tongue for fear of what she might ask Hannah before she was ready to talk about it.

Beside her, Hannah remained stone-faced and reeling. Despite their best intentions, they soon entered traffic so thick that it made it difficult to go more than thirty-five miles an hour. Within a half-hour, they were completely stopped on the highway.

"Well, this is some start to the trip, isn't it?" Angie tried to break the silence.

Hannah made a soft sound in her throat.

"You always hated when we had to drive through Indiana," Angie tried to joke.

"Ha."

Angie's stomach tightened. How could she dig into what had happened between Hannah and Gary? And would she sit in a car with a quiet Hannah for the next eighteen hours?

"I hate traffic." Angie recognized how boring the words were yet couldn't take them back.

"Hmm," Hannah returned.

Angie's phone began to buzz. She grabbed it and read JANICE on the screen.

"We don't have to get that right now," Angie said.

"Let's just answer it. Get it out of the way," Hannah said firmly. She answered the call and put it on speaker. For a long moment, nobody said anything, and there was only the sound of static.

"Janice?" Angie tried. "Are you there?"

"Angela, hello," Janice said. "I was hoping to catch you. How is Chicago?"

"Good," Angie said, not wanting to dig into the specifics of their current location. "What's wrong?"

"Hi, Grandma," Hannah called into the phone.

Janice's voice grew soft and surprised. "Hannah! Oh goodness me, I didn't know you'd be there. How are you doing, sweetheart?"

"Just fine, Grandma. I'm so sorry that I missed the funeral." Hannah's voice wavered, threatening tears.

"Darling, I'm sure your grandfather knows how much you love him," Janice told her, sounding on the verge of a breakdown as well. "We'll see each other soon, honey. I'm sure of it."

Hannah pressed her fingers into her eyes and let a soft sob escape. Angie glanced worriedly at her daughter as she inched through traffic, praying for release. With Janice on the phone,

Hannah full-on broken, and bad traffic, it felt like one of those levels in a horror game.

"Now, Angela. I wanted to discuss something the lawyer set up," Janice continued. "Based on your father's will, he wanted to create a fund for foster children in the state of Ohio. He set aside an enormous amount for this very fund."

"Wow, Janice," Angie heard herself say, although she wasn't entirely sure how she felt about it.

"I think it's only fitting, don't you? He had such a heart for children from broken homes. It's just broken me to pieces, knowing that he adopted you at such a young age. He never told me about it. Hannah, can you believe that?"

"I can't," Hannah told her stiffly.

"I've forgotten the best part of it," Janice continued. "He wanted to call it the Hannah Fund, after his greatest love, his grandchild."

"Wow, Grandma." Hannah began doubtfully.

"Naturally, I'll have more specifics to go over in the coming weeks," Janice continued. "And I will want both of you to be involved as much as possible, especially you, Angela. After all you've been through. I've thought so much about your birth mother and about what she went through when she gave you up." Janice clucked her tongue absently. "Well, anyway. I'll let you girls go. Let me know when you can make another trip to Cincinnati. Don't make this old lady drive up to the big city. You know it terrifies me."

Janice hung up after that and left Angie and Hannah in another of their impenetrable silences. The traffic was thick as molasses; they hadn't moved further than one hundred feet in twenty minutes. There must have been an accident.

"The Hannah Fund," Angie finally said, wanting to make space for some kind of conversation. "What do you think about that?"

But suddenly, Hannah finally gave in to her full-flung emotions and burst into tears. She covered her palms across her face and wailed as her body convulsed with sorrow.

"Hannah! Hannah! Breath, baby." Angie placed her hand on Hannah's shoulder and tried to steady her. But Hannah's wails still wouldn't calm.

"I just... I just..." Hannah dropped her chin onto her chest. "I can't believe I didn't go to his funeral."

Angie's heart split in two. She tried to reach Hannah's hand but couldn't make it.

"Hannah, honey. He wasn't there," Angie pointed out.

Hannah grumbled. "I know that. But I loved him. I loved my grandfather, and now he's gone. And if he even knew what kind of life I've built for myself... He would be so ashamed of me."

"Honey! He wouldn't be ashamed of you. Your grandfather loved everything about you," Angie protested.

Hannah shook her head almost violently. A hiccup escaped her throat. "Mom... Oh, Mom. I don't know what I've done with my life. I don't know why I'm here."

Angie placed her teeth on her bottom lip, at a loss of what to say. She wanted to reach over and stroke Hannah's hair the way she had when she was a child.

"What happened, Hannah?" Angie whispered. "Honey, you can talk to me. I'll help you in any way I can. I'm always here for you. I promise you that."

Hannah blew her nose into a tissue and dropped her head back on the car seat. "It all started last spring. I was failing two courses because I couldn't get up in time for class. Maybe it was depression or anxiety or just loneliness. I don't know. I met a group of girls in the dance department who barely scraped by and partied all weekend and into Monday or Tuesday morning, sometimes. I loved being with them. I loved that they didn't seem to care about anything. My music school friends seemed so boring to me. They were always immersed in school, always practicing. I felt like I'd practiced my entire life away, and nothing was ever going to happen to me because of it."

"That's understandable," Angie whispered, inwardly cursing herself for pushing Hannah so far into music. Maybe she'd never liked it to begin with?

"Don't get me wrong," Hannah added. "I always loved music. But I started to wonder if I was even good at it. And the dance girls didn't seem to care if they were good at dancing at all. They came from rich families. Their lives were set. And they had the greatest parties." Hannah puffed out her cheeks.

"Last summer was when it really picked up. I met some guys who hung around the girls who were into dance. They introduced me to a lot of things... Things I'm not so proud I did. And they also introduced me to Gary. Gary, Gary, Gary..." Hannah shook her head sadly. "He seemed so good at first. So kind. He asked me why I was wasting my life doing something I wasn't even so sure I wanted to do? And one night, when we stayed up till six in the morning talking, I just spontaneously emailed my advisor and dropped out of the next semester. At first, I thought it would give me some time to think things over."

Angie couldn't speak. She could visualize it: a terribly young and talented woman falling in love with a young man with such power over her.

"And heck, maybe I really did need to think," Hannah continued, her voice catching. "I have to tell you; there were many moments last semester when I really missed music school. It hurt me so bad not to talk to you and not to talk to Dad. I was just so ashamed of what I'd done. I practiced around the house when Gary went to work, but I could just feel myself getting so much worse than I had been. It was depressing."

"Honey, it really hasn't been that long," Angie whispered. "Just six months or so. You could easily get back at it."

"Not now, Mom," Hannah whispered.

"Why not?" Angie demanded.

Hannah groaned and placed her hands over her eyes once more. The traffic picked up slightly, forcing Angie to press on the gas and rush around a semi-truck.

"I'm such an idiot, Mom," Hannah continued, wailing.

"Come on, honey. Don't call yourself that. You're not."

"I am..." Hannah dropped her head toward her thighs and groaned. "I don't even know how to tell you this. I wanted to leave Gary. Back in October, already, I was all set to leave. But early November, I took a test..."

Hannah stopped talking. A big black truck drove around them, blaring its horn. Angie wanted to curse at the driver. Her heart pounded loudly in her ears. She knew, now, what came next. She knew, now, why Hannah hadn't had the strength to leave Gary and why she hadn't come to the funeral in the first place.

"I'm pregnant," Hannah whispered then. "Three months along. So, there's that."

Again, the traffic stopped short. Angie was suddenly conscious that she wasn't just transporting Hannah any longer, but also her future grandchild! She immediately told herself to drive as carefully as she could and sucked in a deep breath to calm herself down.

Now, stopped in traffic, Angie took her daughter's hand gently in hers and made eye contact.

"Honey, you're pregnant!" Angie whispered, her voice lilting with excitement.

"Yay, me. I'm pregnant," Hannah breathed, sounding devastated.

"It's the most magical thing in the world," Angie told her firmly. "And I'm going to help you with everything, every step of the way, as long as you'll let me."

Hannah closed her eyes as tears rolled down her cheeks.

She then flew herself across the vehicle and wrapped her arms around her mother. The two of them— Hannah, and Angie, sat wordless and hopeful in the middle of traffic in Northern Indiana. They were the daughter, granddaughter and great-grandchild of Wendy and Glenn Barrington, people they might never know. How strange life was.

Chapter Seventeen

Luke was grateful to have Heather on the plane on the way back. It was such a contrast to his flight from Bangor to NYC, during which fear of flying and fear of what Heather might say once he arrived had competed for the biggest fear of all. Comfort had been the furthest thing from his mind. Now, with Heather's hand in his as she studied a magazine that was strewn out across her lap, and an entire future before them, Luke could breathe easier. Maybe flying wouldn't always be his favorite way to travel. But right then, it didn't matter at all.

It devastated Luke to say goodbye to Heather at the airport. Apparently, she had a meeting with her agent in Portland that morning, and he'd pledged himself to the Acadia Eatery for later that afternoon.

"Maybe we can meet up tonight?" he asked after he kissed her with his eyes closed.

"Sure, that sounds nice. After your shift?"

"That sounds good to me," Luke breathed. He wanted to tell her that she intoxicated him, that his love for her was the single greatest feeling he'd achieved in his life. But such things weren't entirely appropriate in the grim shadows of an airport parking lot. "I'll see you later, Heather."

"Thanks again for your surprise visit," Heather whispered as she placed her nose directly on his. "I have a feeling it changed our lives for the better."

Luke walked on air for the next several hours. He drove back in a daydream state, singing the lyrics for every song on the radio, even the tunes he didn't really like. When he reached the Acadia Eatery that afternoon, he blared the radio as he chopped vegetables, getting all the busboys, waiters, waitresses, and even Nicole in on his game. They howled out the lyrics for Toto's "Africa," which Luke punctuated with precise "chop" sounds with his razor-sharp knife.

"Someone had a pretty good trip," Casey noted from the doorway, her arms folded over her chest.

"I saw you on TV," Nicole told him. "And I screamed."

"You didn't tell us you were going!" Casey cried.

"I know…" Luke shook his head mischievously. "The idea just kind of came to me. And then suddenly, I was there."

"Spontaneous Luke," Nicole teased.

"I hope you guys held down the fort without me here?"

"As if we need you at all, Luke," Casey quipped before she disappeared back into the foyer.

"She's been surprisingly kind to the guests lately," Nicole said with a smile. "But I guess she'll reserve her sharp tongue for special moments." She then widened her grin to add, "Heather told us what happened, by the way."

Luke's cheeks burned red with embarrassment. "I just couldn't leave it the way it was."

"I don't think the confusing nature of it was good for either of you," Nicole said softly. "But I also think it's so incredible of you to allow her space to think about what she wants. Especially after everything she went through."

"Thank you, Nicole," Luke murmured. "That means a lot."

"My sister can be a confusing one," Nicole finished. "But she means the world to me. And I know you're one of the only people in the world who's worthy of her. That's saying something."

* * *

After the dinner rush cleared out, Luke removed his chef whites, bid goodbye to Nicole and Casey, and headed out into the crisp darkness. The drive back to his house on the coast was so uneventful that he promptly forgot about it the moment he stepped inside. How he ended up seated at the dining room table with the old folder placed before him, he wasn't entirely sure. He hadn't thought of the folder in years.

Luke puffed out his cheeks and opened up the file to find a description of the baby he'd been when his parents had dropped him off all those years before.

BABY - LUKE - BORN FEBRUARY 16, 1978
RECEIVED - FEBRUARY 26, 1978
10 DAYS OLD

Alongside the other bits of information, including his size and weight, was an old black and white photograph of the tiniest of babies. The baby wore only a diaper and had his hands in little fists near his ear. The baby was entirely innocent, at the mercy of his parents. The baby had grown up to be Luke— a little ragged around the edges but happy. Really happy, regardless of everything.

Luke had always suspected that his parents sensed something about him. Something "off." Something that had made them give him away after ten days. Who knows more about you than your parents, especially in the early days?

Luke dropped several logs in his wood-burning fireplace. After another ten minutes, the fire spat gently, casting a warm glow across his living room. Luke sat at the edge of the couch with the folder in his outstretched hands.

Maybe it was time to burn the folder. Maybe it was time to say goodbye completely to the past.

The front door creaked open. Luke turned to find Heather, who'd had a key for several months, stepping in, heeled boot first. A smile stretched from ear to ear, and her cheeks were crimson from the chill.

"Hi," she greeted sweetly.

Luke leaped up, the folder still in hand, and headed over to kiss her. Their kiss lasted until Heather tittered with laughter and dropped her head back.

"What are you up to?" she asked.

"I was thinking about doing my two favorite things," Luke confessed. "Sitting by the fire and kissing my girl."

Heather laughed gently. "Do you want to add wine and snacks to that last?" She lifted her bag and tapped the side.

"Oh, what do you have in there?"

"Sweet and salty popcorn and a killer red wine from a little wine bar in Brooklyn that the girls showed me," Heather informed him.

Luke placed the folder on the coffee table and headed to the kitchen cabinet to find wine glasses. Heather, ever-curious, immediately flipped through the folder to find the old photograph.

"Oh..."

Luke turned quickly to find the woman he loved, captivated with the innocent photo of Luke.

"I want to burn it," Luke announced.

Heather's shoulders dropped. "Luke, I don't know if you really want to do that."

Luke poured two glasses of red and headed for the couch, where he sat with his knees pointed toward the heat of the fire. Heather joined him, placing the folder on his lap.

"It doesn't add anything to my life," Luke said of the folder. "It's just a weight."

Heather sipped her wine thoughtfully. "You could think about all of time as a weight. But isn't it all a matter of perspective?"

"What do you mean?" Luke asked.

"To me, after everything that's happened, it's important to hold all the different stories of my life close and not forget them. They're where I came from. They're why I am the way I am."

Again, Heather opened the folder to peer down at the little ten-year-old baby. Her eyes caught the light of the fire.

"Keep this photograph for him," she whispered, pointing at the photograph. "Because he had it in him to get so far from where he started."

Luke puffed out his cheeks and fell back on the couch. He wasn't entirely sure he believed in what Heather said. She burrowed herself against him and together, they watched the fire for the next several moments, both lost in their own thought.

"You know what I keep thinking about this place?" Heather asked softly.

"What?"

Heather cocked her head and eyed the living room. "I keep thinking that it needs a spruce-up."

"What do you mean?" Luke asked, his smile crooked.

"This cottage needs a facelift in a bad way," Heather confessed. "Which means it's just about as wind-torn and salt-torn as anything else. Even the inside... the kitchen cupboards need refurbishing. And the walls! Don't you think you should repaint them?"

Luke laughed. "You have quite a few ideas, I see."

Heather grabbed a pad of paper and a pen. "I'm not Casey

the Architect. But I do have a flair for interior design. You should see my place back in Portland."

She stumbled over her words, then, and blinked back up at Luke. After a monumental pause, she added, "By the way. I've been thinking about putting the house there on the market."

"Wow. That's a big step."

"It really is," Heather breathed. "Especially after that whole speech I just made about holding onto your past. That house has so many memories. I raised my girls there. I had a real love there. But maybe there's something to be said about embracing the future as well. Sure, you can hold onto the photographs. The little things..." she added, pointing at the folder. "But you can allow the big things, the things that weigh you down, to slip away."

The fire continued to crackle gently. Heather burrowed herself against his chest. She gave a gentle drumbeat to his thigh, one that matched his heartbeat.

"I can help you with anything you need," Luke told her gently. "When it comes to selling the old house."

"Thank you," Heather whispered. "That means a lot."

Again, silence. There was a density to it, proof that they were both busy with their own chaotic thoughts. After only a minute more, however, Heather said, "Now, do you want to try that sweet and salty popcorn? Or what?" She jumped up from the couch to retrieve the snacks as Luke cackled with laughter.

He wasn't sure where his life would be if it wasn't for her. She'd become his everything.

Chapter Eighteen

Sixty-five miles outside of Massachusetts, the sunset began to ooze into oranges and pinks in the rearview mirror. It was day two of their "mother-daughter" road trip, and since the initial confession of Hannah's pregnancy, the two women had gotten on like gangbusters. A smattering of empty snack wrappers lined the floor in front of Hannah's seat. She had crossed her legs beneath her and removed her sweatshirt so that Angie caught the tiny three-month baby bump. The radio stations outside of Massachusetts played hits from Hannah's teenage years, songs that, back then, Hannah and Angie had sung in Hannah's bedroom as they'd tried out things like purple eyeliner and high-heeled sandals.

"I can't believe we have only one more day left before we arrive," Angie said as she adjusted her foot somewhere beneath her torso. This was how she'd sat as a teenager, driving through Cincinnati, on the hunt for trouble.

"I know," Hannah breathed. "What do you think you'll say to Luke the first time you see him?"

Angie's heart lifted. "How crazy this situation is, but how happy I am to have found him."

They continued to drive. The sun dipped further and further toward the horizon line. Angie's hands on the wheel turned the color of blood orange.

Suddenly, Hannah blurted, "I think I want to tell Gary it's officially over."

Angie's ears began to ring. This was it. Maybe everything could go back to how it had been, with the addition of an adorable baby.

Since Hannah's story, Angie hadn't pressed Hannah for more details— not about Gary, not about prenatal vitamins, not about anything. Rather, she'd decided to push those conversations to other times. It was better to treasure the here-and-now of their road trip, a time she would surely never get back.

"Do you want to talk about this?" Angie finally asked.

"I just can't help but think... for any other girl, Gary would have just been a phase, you know? But I was stupid enough to let him be the father of my baby."

"Not stupid, Hannah. Never stupid." Maybe the better word was "reckless." At twenty years old, being reckless was the name of the game, sometimes. Angie certainly had had her times.

"Yeah, well. It's not like he'll ever be able to offer me anything like child support. Or emotional support. He doesn't know how to love properly. I know he comes from a rough family. That he isn't exactly programmed to be considerate. But that isn't the kind of man I want around my baby."

Angie repositioned her hands on the steering wheel. "How do you think he'll take the news?"

Hannah nodded. "He'll put up a fight at first, but it'll only be for show. He has no idea how to handle this, either and besides, you must have heard how the two of us rip into each other. We have no real love for each other. I don't know if we ever really did."

After that, Hannah seemed resistant to conversation. She steamed in her own thoughts as Angie continued to drive them east. After nightfall, Angie suggested that they hit up a motel in the area, one rather close to a beach. After they checked in, Hannah, resolute, told her mother that she wanted to head out to the beach to give Gary a call. "It's time," she explained. "I don't want to wait any longer."

Angie nodded and watched as her daughter slipped out and headed for the star-filled night sky above the frothing ocean. Angie grabbed the keys to the motel room and headed into the sterile and tan-colored motel room. A small window had an "ocean view," which made the room seven dollars more than some of the other motel rooms. Angie searched through her bag for her cleanser and night creams, wanting to prep for the night and then collapse in bed. As she read the instructions on her newly-purchased night cream, her phone buzzed in her pocket.

It was Felix calling her.

The name confused Angie for a number of reasons. Number one: what did Felix have to say to her? Hadn't he moved on with Autumn and the jazz band? Didn't he have the apartment all to himself for his newfound affair?

Number two: his name on the screen reminded Angie that she'd hardly thought of him at all the past week or so. After her father's death and her reunion with Hannah, Angie wasn't sure, exactly, what there was to think about her impending divorce. Maybe it was just a chance to start over.

Curiosity, maybe, led her to answer the phone.

"Hello?

"Hi, Ang." Felix used his dark tone of voice, the one he used when he entered a "do not mess around with me right now, I'm thinking" phase. Angie knew the voice well.

"Hi, Felix," she echoed.

Silence.

Angie yawned quietly and glanced at herself in the mirror. Strangely, she'd gotten something of a tan from the hours at the wheel, despite the fact that it was early February.

"Angie, I wanted to know if I could get your opinion about something. See... In 'Ain't Misbehavin', we always have that key change and then the improv piano solo. And you always did something pretty specific in bar nine of the solo. Something that made the crowd go wild."

Ah. Felix had called because he needed to give the new pianist her tricks of the trade.

"Yeah. It goes up to G sharp minor," Angie said flippantly. "But she's got to make sure she plays it staccato. That's what brings the crowd to their knees."

"Marvelous, Ang. Really. Wow. I knew you'd know it in a heartbeat."

"I probably played that song a thousand times," Angela returned. "I'll be playing it in my coffin."

Felix laughed overly long at her bad joke. Angie itched to get off the phone and go check on Hannah. At least, she thought now it wasn't like Gary could hurt Hannah from so far away. Words were nothing.

"I guess you can guess already that our new pianist ain't nothing compared to our old pianist," Felix continued.

"Is that so?"

"Yeah. It's been hard to get her up to speed on a lot of the tracks. I'd ask you to come in and sit with her to help out, but then, I guess, I'd just have you play the numbers instead."

Angie was not amused.

"Yeah. Well. The thing is, Angie. A lot of things have happened over the past month. Enough to make a guy think about what his life is and where that life is going."

"I see."

"And you have every right to be angry with me, Ang. Every right. I messed up in a big way and destroyed the only thing important to me. And there's no reason you should ever forgive me."

Angie rolled her eyes into the back caverns of her head. Were men always so weak?

"It's basically over with Autumn," he continued. "She's never meant anything to me. But you and me— we had it all. We started this jazz ensemble from the very beginning. We— we had such a life together."

Had he been in the room, Angie could have thrown something in his face. She brought the curtain up from over the small window as Hannah hung up her phone and headed in from the beach.

"It's just that I don't think I even like playing music as much as I used to," Felix whispered, his voice rasping. "And everyone at every jazz club asks about you. It's been debilitating to me. Knowing that you're out there somewhere. Knowing you're probably not even playing because of my infidelity."

Angie wanted to ask him what it mattered to him, whether she played the piano or not. But at that moment, there was a knock on the hotel room. Angie rushed to let her daughter in. Hannah's cheeks were tinged red, but not a tear had fallen.

"I have to let you go," Angie said to Felix, careful not to show any emotion in her tone. "I'll have to think about everything you said. Have a good night." She hung up and allowed her daughter to crumple forward upon her.

"He said so many terrible things," Hannah whispered into Angie's shoulder.

"I know, honey. But you never have to see him again if you don't want to," Angie told her in the softest voice. "Let his words roll off you like waves and focus on the future. It's all you can do."

Chapter Nineteen

Hannah sat at the very center of her double bed in a pair of pajama shorts and a big Cincinnati Reds t-shirt, which her grandfather had purchased for her tenth birthday. At the time, she'd joked that she could wear the t-shirt as a dress. Now, she joked that she could wear it as maternity clothing.

Angie performed her night-cream ritual as Hannah watched from the bed. "That's a lot of cream and serum," she told her mother.

"You'll be just like me soon," Angie returned. "The act of self-preservation begins with a night-time ritual. Well, I take that back. It actually begins with self-respect. That's something you seem to have in spades. It's taken me a long time to figure out how to have respect for myself. Maybe I still don't completely have it."

When Angie returned to the double-bed opposite Hannah's in the motel room, Hannah elaborated a bit more on what Gary had said over the phone. "He says if I ever come crying to him about what I need for the baby, he'll tell me, 'I told you so,' and hang up."

"What a child," Angie returned.

Angie considered telling Hannah about the phone call she'd just received from Felix. But if she wasn't sure what she felt about it, then how could she share it with her twenty-year-old daughter? Beyond that, it was a sure thing that Hannah didn't exactly feel great about her parents divorcing. Angie didn't want to complicate things anymore by asking her daughter's opinion on the fact that Felix wanted to try again.

"I just feel so pathetic for having fallen for this bad boy," Hannah continued. "I don't know what came over me last summer, but I should have known that it never ends well. I wish I could take it all back."

Angie dropped down from the bed and walked over to Hannah, where she curled around her daughter and held her as she wept. Before Angie knew what she'd done, she began to describe a similar time period of her life— a time she now saw so differently after twenty-five years of experience.

"I know you did the right thing," Angie whispered. "Because I know what it's like to fall in love with someone who is problematic. And I know what it's like to have him break your heart."

Hannah dropped her chin to her chest. "You're talking about Dad."

"I love your father, Hannah. I've always loved him. And he was a brilliant father to you, which I always respected. But if I'm honest with myself, there were red flags right and left when we first got together. He always flirted with other women and made me feel very small. I always felt like if he met another woman who was better at music than me, he would run out the door just as quickly as anything. It's difficult for me to really remember those times, especially because your dad and I really did build a beautiful life together for a while. But what I'm saying is this. Maybe, romantically, I should have trusted my gut. The way you are right now."

Hannah's eyes were round as orbs. She placed a hand across her pregnant belly and heaved a sigh, one of relief mixed with fear. "Thank you for saying that, Mom." She then swallowed and added, "I just keep thinking about this baby. This baby, my baby. And how much I already love this baby."

"It happens so early, doesn't it?" Angie whispered.

"I guess so." Hannah shook her head, incredulous. "I cannot imagine what mother could ever give up her baby."

Angie nodded knowingly yet didn't have the strength to speak.

"I already know that I want to love this baby in every way possible," Hannah continued. "And I would never give them up. Not in a million years."

Angie placed her head on Hannah's shoulder and exhaled all the air from her lungs. "I have to believe my parents had good reason to give me up," Angie said.

"I just can't imagine it," Hannah said doubtfully.

Angie raised her head to catch Hannah's eyes. "Your grandfather would be so, so proud of what you did today."

"Breaking up with my loser boyfriend?"

"No. You took ownership of your life. You've taken the first step toward becoming a full, confident, powerful woman. He loved you with everything he had, Hannah. Probably, he always knew what kind of woman you would be."

Chapter Twenty

Early February was something of a cozy era for the Keating Inn and Acadia Eatery. The Acadia Mountains, seen from within the Eatery, were glossy with snow. Frenchman Bay frothed against the docks while the Atlantic beyond was dark as ink. Bar Harbor itself looked like a postcard, its multi-colored buildings cutesy, with leftover Christmas wreaths and lights in various corners, either forgotten or purposefully left up.

Luke walked through the center of town with his hand stuffed in his pockets as a sharp breeze blew off the bay and made his eyes water. As the Keating Inn was only half-booked today, Nicole, Heather, and Casey had plotted a special Bar Harbor Guests only feast that night at the Acadia Eatery, with an elaborate multi-course meal that would begin at seven and continue on until ten. The Harvey Sisters had such tremendously big hearts, especially for their newly-adopted community. Luke felt so connected to them. He also beamed with confidence that came from falling in love. He'd forgotten what that felt like.

As Luke headed toward the Keating Inn and Acadia Eatery to prep for the night ahead, he found himself greeting nearly every passer-by with a big smile and a friendly, "Hey there. How are you doing?" The smiles he received back were bright, but laced with confusion. "What's gotten into Luke lately?" seemed the question on everyone's lips. "He's in love," was the only appropriate answer.

Abby stood at the front desk of the Keating Inn, her brow furrowed as she clacked her fingers across the computer keyboard. Abby took her job seriously, sometimes too seriously, and Luke liked to tease her about this.

"You saving the world over there, Abby?"

Abby groaned inwardly yet didn't move her eyes from the computer screen. "You know it."

"You know what else I know?" Luke asked. "You're only, what, twenty-three? You should be out there, getting into the Bar Harbor scene."

Abby finally pulled her gaze from the computer. "What's that got to do with anything?"

Luke wanted to tell her how much she might regret this time period of her life— these hours wasted at work and then at home, chatting with her mother and aunts as though she never needed to build a life of her own.

"Oh nothing," Luke replied with a shrug. "I just hope you're liking it here in Bar Harbor."

"Happier than ever," Abby returned, not bothering to wear a smile. "I just made an online post about the dinner tonight. Looking like mostly everyone will be able to attend."

"Great news," Luke told her. "Is your mom here already?"

"Of course," Abby said. "She's been obsessing about the menu since she woke up this morning."

"That's our Nicole." He then headed back to the kitchen, where he found Nicole nearly tugging every strand from her head as she finalized the last elements of the menu based on what she had in the kitchen already. Nicole was very anti-waste, which Luke appreciated.

"Okay. Want to hear the menu?" Nicole asked, her eyes wide due to nerves.

"Nicole. Why are you so nervous? You're giving people free dinner. They'd love it even if it was chicken nuggets with French fries. Actually, they might love it more," Luke countered. He grabbed an apple from a large bowl of fruit and tore off a large bite. It tasted better than any apple he'd ever eaten. Again: love made things better.

"You think they'd like chicken nuggets more?" Nicole demanded, stricken.

Luke forced himself to center his focus. "Let me hear the menu."

Nicole cleared her throat and dove into her description for the night's courses. "We start with an avocado bruschetta," she began. "Followed by cream cheese and walnut-stuffed dates. After that, we have a quinoa tomato-cucumber salad, followed by an entree of chicken parmigiana and a cheesecake dessert."

Luke whistled, impressed.

"You think it's good enough?" Nicole asked.

"You know it's good enough," Luke affirmed. "You don't need to ask me."

Casey rushed into the kitchen after that to ensure that all guests for the night had confirmed. Luke ate the rest of his refreshing apple, tossed the cork in the trash, and then scrubbed his hands clean. He needed to prep the bruschetta so that they'd be easily shoved in the oven, then prep the dates, the walnuts, the cream cheese, the chicken, the tomato, and the quinoa. Nicole would start the cheesecake as soon as possible, as it required a number of hours to bake and then cool. After about twenty minutes, Luke, Nicole, and several other members of the kitchen staff became like a well-oiled machine.

Heather texted around six that she, Kristine, and Bella had

finished their downtown shopping and would head into the Keating Inn and Acadia Eatery for glasses of wine before dinner. Luke's heart jumped with excitement.

LUKE: Can't wait to see you.

LUKE: Nicole's got us working to death.

HEATHER: She's the best. You'd better listen to her.

LUKE: I always do. (Too scared not to.)

Luke headed out to the bathroom and then walked back into the kitchen through the back door. From there, he had a view through the window of the back office, where to his immense surprise, he spotted Nicole and none other than Evan Snow. Evan Snow leaned Nicole back over the desk and kissed her with reckless abandon. It looked as though they might break the desk beneath them or at least fall right onto it.

Luke looked away, and forced himself forward, back to his cutting board. A couple of minutes later, Nicole emerged, red-faced and embarrassed. There was no sign of Evan. He'd probably escaped through the back door.

"How's it going?" Nicole asked casually.

"Good," Luke told her, hardly lifting his head. He was terrified that his eyes would give away what he'd seen.

Heather and Luke had talked quite a bit about the budding Evan and Nicole relationship. Heather hadn't been very sure of what she thought of it. After all, Evan was renowned as "the evilest man in all of Bar Harbor." In the same breath, they had Evan Snow to thank for making sure the Keating Inn and Acadia Eatery remained in the hands of the Harvey Sisters.

"Plus," Heather had added a few nights before. "Nicole deserves a little romance in her life. She's been so hungry to prove herself in that restaurant. I hope she finds a little 'me time,' too."

Now that Heather and Luke were "official," he wondered if Nicole and Evan would come out with the "official" nature of their relationship, as well. He hoped they wouldn't always hide behind closed doors. Clearly, there was something about Evan Snow that the others couldn't comprehend— something that Nicole had fallen head-over-heels for.

That said, if they never wanted to reveal their relationship and what they felt about one another, that was their business. People did what they needed to do to survive. Luke knew that better than most.

There was a light knock at the kitchen door before it swung open to reveal the beautiful Heather Harvey. Luke forgot all about the tomatoes beneath his knife. He dropped everything and headed over to greet her, his heart somewhere in his throat. He kissed her, right there in the doorway, in front of Nicole and the rest of the staff and even God himself. When their kiss broke, she blinked dewy eyes up at him and said, "Wow. What a greeting."

"Only the best at the Acadia Eatery," Luke told her.

"Do you greet all your guests like that?" Heather arched an eyebrow playfully.

Luke turned his gaze toward Nicole, whose cheeks now burned an even deeper crimson. "We do, actually," Luke returned with a sly grin.

Nicole ducked back into the office and disappeared from sight.

"She seems stressed," Heather noted.

"She'll make it. The menu's perfect, and everyone's agreed to come," Luke told her. "It should be a very simple, easy night. No surprises."

"No surprises," Heather affirmed, drawing her hands across the white fabric on his shoulders. "Thank goodness."

Chapter Twenty-One

"Mom! You've got to be kidding me."

Angie and Hannah hovered at a red light on the outskirts of Bar Harbor, Maine and took in this splendorous view of a village on the stony edge of the continent, so far from the Chicago home they'd left behind. Each building seemed transplanted from a storybook, bright with yellows, pinks, and blues. Frenchman Bay beamed out toward the impenetrable Atlantic Ocean, and the Acadia Mountains surged above them, peppered white with snow and dark green with pine trees.

"It's like another planet," Angie whispered.

"Do you think there are whales out there?" Hannah asked, pointing toward the ocean beyond.

"I'm sure there's a whole lot more than that." Angie lifted her foot from the brake as the red light shifted back to green. "Do you still have the directions up? We need to find the Keating Inn."

It was seven-thirty in the evening, and Angie and Hannah had been on the road for three days. Their legs were fatigued and useless and their stomachs bubbled strangely from salty snacks and diner food. They were ready for a warm, comfortable bed that wasn't associated with a hotel and some hot, wholesome food.

"There's the inn!" Hannah pointed at the gorgeous old-world mansion, white with black shutters, located on a hill overlooking Frenchman Bay. "Gosh, it's prettier than the pictures, isn't it?"

Angie's heart sped up. The Keating Inn parking lot sign flipped around with the sharp winter breeze. She pulled right and parked in the gravel side of the lot, then blinked up at the beautiful house.

She'd just driven nineteen hours based on the half-idea that the man they'd seen on television was her long-lost brother. Was she insane? But when she turned her gaze toward Hannah, she found a beautiful, vibrant, and curious woman, who now whipped on her winter coat and asked her mother excitedly, "Should we go in?" Perhaps this trip hadn't been about Luke and her long-lost parents at all. Perhaps it had all been about Hannah.

"All right. Let's do it," Angie told her with assurance. "But remember. We said we weren't going to get our hopes up."

"Right," Hannah confirmed with a nod. "Besides, maybe they have space at the inn. We can sleep in one of those cozy beds, eat a ton of food, and explore Bar Harbor before we drive back."

Angie and Hannah stepped out of the car, took deep breaths, and then breathed out bright white steam. Unconsciously, Hannah splayed her hand across her stomach and stepped toward the front door as Angie followed.

The foyer of the Keating Inn was beautiful, with mahogany walls, thick, handwoven rugs, and paintings from another era. Antique desks and chairs made up a large seating area, complete with a fireplace that now crackled and spat against its final logs.

"Where is everyone?" Hannah asked as she looked around.

"I have no idea." Angie swatted the bell on the front desk to alert someone. They waited for a good minute before Hannah pointed to the hallway that led out of the foyer and deeper into the estate.

"There's a sign that says Eatery over there," Hannah said. "Maybe everyone's there?"

Angie could hardly breathe as they stepped toward the hallway and headed toward a pair of double-wide doors. As they approached, the roar behind the doors grew louder, proof that a number of people existed beyond— probably in the midst of one of the Harvey Sister's elaborate meals.

Just before they reached the front door, a waiter whipped open the door, prepared to speed past them. He stumbled and blinked at them, confused.

"Can I help you?" he asked politely.

"We were just wondering if we could have a table," Hannah inquired. "We haven't checked in yet, but we're starving."

The waiter turned around to investigate the packed dining room. From the doorway, it looked like the most marvelous feast. Husbands and wives, large families, lovers and friends sat around beautifully-set dining room tables and nourished themselves with conversation and what looked to be some kind of salad. Their wine glasses caught the light from the hanging chandelier, and laughter rang out musically, echoing against the far window.

"Wow," Hannah breathed.

"Actually, there's a two-top over here," the waiter said hurriedly. "We're serving a special menu tonight, but we have plenty of leftovers. I can get you set up. Wine for both of you?"

"Just water, please," Angie told him.

"Perfect. Makes it easy on me," the waiter told them as he led them toward one lonely table, a bit further away from the rest of the diners. "The chef invited a number of guests tonight to thank them for their loyalty over the harsher winter months."

"That's beautiful," Angie returned as she sat, watching as the waiter set the table with china plates and glowing water glasses. Hannah sat across from her and eyed the rest of the dining room.

"Is Luke working tonight?" Hannah asked suddenly.

Angie tried to kick Hannah under the table, but missed.

"He is, actually." The waiter's eyes widened with excitement. "Are you friends with him?"

"Kind of," Hannah told him.

"He's super busy right now, but I'm sure you could catch him after dessert," the waiter explained. "Now, I'll be right back with your water and your first course. Avocado bruschetta!"

"Oh gosh." Hannah let out a sigh. "Real food!"

The waiter sped away, leaving Angie and Hannah alone at the table. Angie huffed and said, "Did you have to ask him about Luke?"

"Don't you think it's good to just bite the bullet?" Hannah asked.

Angie groaned inwardly. "I'm terrified."

"Food will give us courage," Hannah told her mother. "And besides. What did we say already about not getting our hopes up?"

"Boy, you sure are wise for your years, honey." Angie blinked toward the kitchen door, which swiveled out and then back in again before it revealed none other than Heather Harvey Talbot, who held a large pitcher of ice water and grinned out across the massive group of diners.

"There's Heather," Angie whispered.

"Oh!" Hannah whipped around excitedly. "It's like seeing a celebrity."

The waiter arrived back with his own pitcher of water, plus two servings of avocado bruschetta. Little green slices of avocado were lined across the crusty slice of bread, and pomegranate seeds flickered across, terrifically bright.

"It looks incredible!" Hannah cried. "We've lived off of chips and pretzels the past few days."

The waiter laughed. "I know the feeling. Since I came to work here, I've had every kind of vegetable and fruit known to man. It goes against my very exclusive teenage boy diet."

He sped away. Hannah tore into her avocado bruschetta and closed her eyes to the first bite. Angie lifted her first forkful and glanced across the dining room to watch Heather Harvey Talbot as she paused to speak with a six-person table. She had the air of always caring very deeply about whatever someone told her, even if it was something simple about the weather. She then walked across the dining room and stopped again at a four-person table, where twin girls sat across from one another and beamed up at Heather. These were the girls from the talk show— Heather's daughters. Heather placed a hand on one of their shoulders and gestured across the dining room with the full pitcher, clearly talking about the crowd.

"It kind of feels like we entered into a private world where we don't belong," Angie told Hannah.

Hannah swallowed her food and shrugged. "It's fascinating, isn't it? To run away from the problems in our life and spy on other people like this. Nobody knows our name anywhere east of Cincinnati or west of Chicago. We're strangers. Well, until you meet Luke. Did you bring the folder inside?"

Angie nodded yet felt foolish. What was the plan? Would she just run into the back kitchen and throw the folder at him? Her hands shook so much that she had to put the fork and knife back down.

The waiter arrived with the second course, walnut and cream-filled dates. He then took Hannah's plate away while eyeing Angie's.

"Is there something wrong with the food?" he asked Angie.

"No. It's delicious."

He nodded, then disappeared back into the kitchen. Angie eyed the whipping door to try to catch sight of Luke somewhere back there. She spotted a woman in chef's whites, maybe one of the Harvey Sisters, before the door closed again. Before long, the waiter arrived back with a serving of quinoa salad, which Hannah pounced on. Again, Angie hadn't managed to eat the entirety of her plate.

"This is really delicious, Mom," Hannah said.

"You can have some of mine," Angie insisted. "I'm too nervous to eat."

Hannah selected one of her stuffed dates and ate it contemplatively, watching the crowd. Angie followed Hannah's gaze to find Heather Harvey not far away, now, standing with one-half of a pitcher of water and a hand on her hip. She eyed Angie and Hannah right back, smiled, and headed straight for them, the pitcher lifted.

Angie's heart nearly exploded with shock. Heather was only five strides away! She grabbed her fork and took an enormous bite of her salad, chewing on the lemony quinoa as Heather lifted the pitcher to refill their water glasses.

"How are you ladies enjoying the dinner?" Heather asked.

"It's insanely good!" Hannah cried.

"Isn't it? My sister's the chef. It was her idea to have this five-course meal for our dearest friends in Bar Harbor. Unfortunately, there weren't enough servers on the schedule tonight, so I'm pitching in with water duties."

"I hope you get a chance to eat," Hannah said.

"Oh yeah. My boyfriend's also back there working away.

He always saves me extra-big servings. The largest slice of cheesecake and the juiciest slab of chicken."

"Lucky you!" Hannah replied, her eyes glittering.

"Yeah, I am lucky," Heather admitted. "By the way, are you ladies staying in the inn? I don't recognize you from Bar Harbor. But maybe I'm mistaken. My memory's not always the most reliable."

Angie and Hannah eyed one another. Again, Angie struggled to kick Hannah under the table, knowing that mischievous glance. Hannah was a live wire and couldn't be trusted.

"Actually... we are! Or, we hope we are," Angie interjected before Hannah could begin. "There wasn't anyone at the front desk to check us in."

"We can fix that after dinner," Heather affirmed. "I'll talk to my niece, Abby. She's usually in charge of that kind of stuff. But right now, I think she's pretty deep into a chicken parmigiana, so. I'll give her space."

Heather gave them a smile that meant she was just about ready to head to another table but wasn't sure how to leave.

"You know..." Hannah began. "I think we saw you on a talk show recently. May?"

Heather's jaw dropped with surprise. "You're kidding! Gosh, yes. I can't believe you saw that."

"You were fantastic," Hannah told her. "I used to read your books when I was younger. They got me through some dark times in my teenage years."

Heather gave her a solemn look. "You have no idea what it means to me to hear that."

"We actually drove all this way because..." Hannah continued.

"Hannah," Angie warned. "Heather has a lot of work to do, I'm sure."

"What?" Heather's brow furrowed. "What are you talking about?"

Hannah's eyes widened toward her mother. "Show her the folder."

Angie bristled. "No, Hannah. We're in the middle of dinner."

"Like you'll be able to eat anyway. Come on. This is the way in," Hannah informed her.

Heather gawked at Angie, then Hannah, then back at Angie. "What folder?" Heather demanded. She then glanced back toward the door to the kitchen, as though she wanted to go grab Luke for protection from these "strangers."

Angie heaved a sigh, reached into her purse, and drew out the old manila folder from over forty years ago.

"What I'm about to say will sound crazy," Angie admitted. "But I recently learned that I was adopted."

Heather's eyes grew clouded with recognition. "I understand how that feels. I guess you heard me talk about it on the talk show."

"Yes, but not only that," Angie continued, her voice wavering. "My birth parents were from Ohio." She then opened the folder onto Glenn Barrington's old driver's license photograph, which offered a mirror-image of Luke, the sous chef in the kitchen.

All the color drained from Heather's face. She placed a hand over her mouth as though she stifled a scream.

"No..." she whispered. "This is crazy... May I look closer?"

Angie nodded. Heather lifted the sheet of paper toward her eyes and studied the image. When her eyes found Angie's again, she asked, "What do you know?"

"Not a lot," Angie told her. "I learned about Glenn and Wendy Barrington very recently. Then, we saw the talk show and discovered this medical file, where Wendy writes about two other children. Leo, two years older than me, and Luke, about a year and half younger than me. Birthday, February 16."

Heather's bottom lip quivered uncontrollably. She swiped her black sleeve over her left eye so that makeup smeared across her cheek.

"I'm so sorry," Heather whispered. "I don't even know what to say."

"You have to ask him if he'd be willing to talk to us," Hannah said. "We've driven from Chicago just to see him."

"And we obviously don't know anything for sure," Angie interjected. "It was a spur of the moment thing, but an important one, no less."

Heather's lips curved into a smile. "I've lived so much of my life based on a whim. Do you mind if I take the photocopy of your father with me to show him?"

Angie could hardly breathe to answer. "Of course."

"But I might wait till after dessert is served if that's okay," Heather explained. "My sister will have my head if I take her sous chef away before we serve everyone."

Angie and Hannah laughed nervously.

"That shouldn't be a problem," Angie told her. "If I don't get a slab of that cheesecake you talked about, I'll be devastated."

Chapter Twenty-Two

"That's a wrap, team." Nicole clapped excitedly as the last platters of caramel cheesecake were whisked out to the twenty-five tables they'd successfully served that night. Luke leaned back against the glossy kitchen counter and removed his chef's hat, his shoulders dropping low. Nicole headed over to him and shook his hand. "Don't know what I would do without you."

"I wish I could say the same," Luke teased. "Actually, I do know. I'd get a whole lot more sleep."

Nicole rolled her eyes as she selected a platter of cheesecake for herself and took a sinful bite. "God, I'm good," she laughed.

"And arrogant, too," Luke returned as he selected a plate for himself.

"As every chef should be," Nicole said.

Luke splayed a tiny piece of cheesecake lined with sticky caramel on his tongue and chewed luxuriously.

"Admit it," Nicole said. "I'm good."

"Okay, okay. You're not bad, kid," Luke told her.

Just then, Heather appeared in the doorway to the kitchen. Her face was strange, paler than Luke had seen it in quite some time. He felt a punch in the gut. Had she changed her mind about him again? Had she stormed in here to tell him it was over?

"Hey, Luke. Can I talk to you in private? Maybe in the office?" Heather asked.

Luke placed his cheesecake on the counter and headed for the office door, unable to speak. Fear coated his tongue. Heather was hot on his heels. When they entered the office, she closed the door firmly behind them. He wanted to scream.

"What's wrong?" Luke's face was marred with confusion. "What is that?"

Heather's hands shook so that the yellowed piece of paper she held quivered between them.

"I just had the strangest conversation," Heather told him. "I don't even know where to begin."

Luke felt slightly lighter. He tilted his head and found her eyes. "You're scaring me."

"I'm sorry," she told him. "I don't even know how to tell you. This woman... She saw us on the talk show. And she'd just discovered this..."

Heather flipped the paper around to show Luke an old photocopy of a driver's license. The man within the square was the spitting image of Luke himself. The name read: GLENN BARRINGTON. And the address: 433 W. TREEHILL RD. OXFORD, OH.

"Heather..." Luke's voice was all over the place. He gaped at this image, at this strange man from Ohio, and at the older design of the driver's license. "What is this?"

"She wants to meet you," Heather whispered. "She has more documents. More things you might want to see."

"Who do you think it is?" Luke demanded. "Or who does she think she is?"

Heather sighed. "There's a possibility she's your sister, Luke. Your sister."

Luke walked like a blind man through the office door and out into the dining room, where the people of Bar Harbor laughed wholeheartedly, tore through their cheesecakes, and drank their wine. He paused at the edge of the dining room, realizing he'd left Heather behind without knowing where he headed. He scanned the dining room as his ears screamed with fear.

A middle-aged woman sat across from a teenage girl toward the right side of the dining room. The teenage girl continued to eat through her cheesecake while the middle-aged woman sat quietly, her hands beneath her chin, waiting. Her eyes turned toward the kitchen door and latched onto him. It seemed like a shiver of recognition passed through them, although Luke couldn't be sure. Suddenly, she stood, and her chair fell back behind her with a loud clatter.

Heather appeared beside him, breathless. "She's seen you. Would you please go talk to her?"

"We can't do it here," Luke told Heather. "Not in the dining room."

"What about the library upstairs," Heather suggested. "It's always empty this time of night."

Luke nodded. Heather wrapped a hand around Luke's elbow and led him toward the woman who remained standing, watching him approach. When he reached her, Luke placed the photocopy of Glenn Barrington on the table between them and brought out a hand to shake hers.

"I'm sorry," he said suddenly. "I don't know quite what to say."

"I'm not one for words right now, either," the woman told him.

The teenager across from the middle-aged woman stood to

greet him. Her smile was warm, inviting. "My mother's been nervous for days."

"I can't imagine why," Luke tried to joke, flashing her a forced smile.

The woman laughed outright, then snapped her lips closed again. "My name is Angela. Angie," she finally said, taking his hand. "I'm sorry for my strange behavior."

"I guess it's to be expected," Luke said. "During this very unexpected occasion." He again studied the photograph of Glenn Barrington, flabbergasted. "I wondered if you wanted to head upstairs to talk for a little while?"

Angie agreed and spoke with the teenager, whom she introduced as Hannah, telling her she would return soon. Hannah said she would eat another two slices of cheesecake by that time. Luke instructed one of the servers that Hannah could eat as many cheesecake slices as she pleased.

"I like him," Hannah told her mother excitedly.

Luke nodded in goodbye to Heather as he led Angie toward the foyer's circular staircase. There, they walked in silence all the way to the top, where they collected themselves on the cozy chairs of the round library. Although it was pitch-dark outside, the light from the inn glowed out, reflecting against the billowing snowflakes that fell from the night sky.

"It's beautiful here," Angie whispered.

"It really is," Luke told her. He again studied her, wondering if they looked like siblings.

Angie flipped open the folder and began to explain what she knew. Her father had recently died and left behind paperwork about her adoption. When she'd spotted Luke on the talk show and compared him to the photograph of her birth father, she'd been mesmerized, yet still doubtful.

"It was this medical document that changed my mind," she said, showing him Wendy Barrington's handwriting which listed a Leo, an Angela, and a Luke as her children.

"That's... that's my birthday," Luke whispered, shocked.

Angie exhaled deeply. "We tracked you down just to see you. Just to tell you what we know. But obviously, there are many possible stories..."

"And you don't have any kind of birth certificate for me?" Luke asked.

"Nothing in the folder," Angie admitted.

"What about death certificates?"

"Nothing in the folder," Angie continued. "And nothing at all about Leo Barrington that I can find. Maybe I just haven't looked hard enough. Or maybe he was adopted, too, and is off somewhere, living some other life. Not knowing he's adopted..."

Luke dropped his head back on the forest-green cushion behind him. Outside, the snow had picked up, frothing beautifully along the window sill.

"Have you ever been to Bar Harbor?" Luke asked her now.

"Never. I've hardly been outside of the Midwest," Angie admitted. "My husband and I were musicians in Chicago for years and years and never had more than rent and a little bit more to keep our lives together. Plus, we always had gigs and could never turn a gig down just to run off somewhere together."

Luke's eyes widened. "A musician?"

Angie blushed. "It sounds stupid to say that. And to be honest with you..." She trailed off for a moment, then continued. "I'm not even playing right now. My husband had an affair with someone in our jazz ensemble. I just found out on New Year's Eve."

"New Year's Eve? Of this past year?"

"A little more than a month ago," Angie admitted. "And since then, I've been, well. Falling apart is maybe the term. My father died on top of it all. And then..."

"You learned about the adoption," Luke confirmed. "And your real parents. And then, maybe, me."

"Maybe even you." Angie shared a sensitive, enthralling smile. She cleared her throat as her eyes watered. "I'm sorry to drag you into my mess like this."

Luke shook his head. "My life's been nothing but a mess since the tenth day after my birth."

"Ten days?"

"That's when they dropped me off. My parents."

"God..." Angie's eyes dropped to the floor. "It looks like I was just a year and a half.. Maybe it was around the same time."

"And then your father adopted you?"

"Yes," Angie said. "And I know how lucky I was for that to happen. I know that the foster system is no picnic."

"No. No, it wasn't."

They shared the silence. Luke again lifted the paper with the list of Wendy Barrington's children: Leo, Angela, and Luke. If this was, in fact, his family, his real family, he tried to imagine some other story, where Wendy and Glenn had raised Leo, Angela, and Luke as their own. What would it have been like to have a brother, four years older? Would Leo have taught Luke the ways of the world? Would Luke have annoyed Leo until they'd become friends later, maybe drinking in bars in Cincinnati through their twenties and then raising families side-by-side? Where would Angie have come into this? Probably, she would have both loved them and hated them, picking fights with their brothers and then, in turn, standing up for them till the bitter end.

That's what family was meant to be. That's what they should have been allowed to be for each other.

Luke's eyes filled with tears again. He blinked them away before returning his gaze to Angie.

"I know," Angie said with a simple shrug.

"What do you know?"

"I just know what it's like. Spiraling into all these different ideas of what life could have been. It's haunted me the past few days. I don't know whether to hate them or find a way to love them," Angie offered.

It was like she'd taken the words directly from Luke's lips.

"Thank you for coming to see me," Luke said suddenly. "My girlfriend and I have had a little bit of a difference in opinion when it comes to discovering the secrets of our past. For her, it was an accident to learn that she was adopted. For me, it was always a fact that I never was adopted. Digging into the past seemed stupid, but with you in front of me, with your very old folder of papers... It all feels a little bit different. Even if we aren't actually siblings. Seeing you here gives me hope."

"Mom? Are you up there?" Hannah called from the staircase.

"Up here, honey!" Angie leaped to her feet to meet her daughter at the top of the steps. There, she hugged her with her eyes closed, exhaling into her.

"I'm tired, Mom," Hannah told her.

"Me too."

Luke jumped to his feet, feeling dizzy "Let me get you a room. We're only half-booked today. Maybe one of our suites is available?"

Downstairs, Abby booked them into one of the "presidential" suites, with a gorgeous view of Frenchman Bay and the Acadia Mountains behind the Keating Inn.

"You're going to have quite a view tomorrow," Abby informed them sleepily as she handed over the antique key. Her lips were tinged with red wine.

"It's taken care of," Luke told Abby from the left of Angie and Hannah.

"Got it," Abby said, noting something on the bill.

"You really don't have to do this, Luke," Angie told him, bowing her head and giving him what Luke could only imagine was a "sister" look.

"I think I do, actually," Luke told her. "Even if you aren't really my sister, you drove all this way to meet me. Nobody's ever done that for me."

Before Angie and Hannah headed up for the night, Luke hugged both of them and wished them well. They exchanged phone numbers so that they could easily communicate over the next few days of their stay.

"Let me know if you need anything at all," Luke told them as he hauled their backpacks and duffel bags up the staircase to the second floor. "I'm always either in the kitchen at Acadia Eatery or just down the road. I can always help."

Chapter Twenty-Three

That night, Luke, Heather, Casey, Grant, and Nicole sat around the kitchen table at the Keating House and reiterated what Luke had learned from Angie and Hannah, who'd driven all the way from Chicago on a wish and a prayer. Luke had taken photographs of the photocopies of Glenn and Wendy Barrington's driver's licenses and the old medical document on which Wendy had written the names LEO, ANGELA, and LUKE, along with the surprising detail of his birth.

Grant, Heather, Casey, and Nicole listened with their eyes widened with shock. When Luke revealed the detail about his birthday, Grant whistled with surprise.

"There are way too many coincidences, don't you think?" Luke asked.

"I mean..." Heather grabbed his phone to look again at the photograph of Glenn, which she positioned alongside Luke's head for the others to see. "Look at this man. Look at them side-by-side. It's uncanny, isn't it?"

"I'm getting a glass of wine," Casey said. "Anyone else?"

Everyone agreed to a glass of Chianti. Casey reappeared from the cabinet with enough wine glasses, which she filled. Everyone else pondered the weight of Luke's story.

"It's not like I have anything she would want to scam me out of," Luke continued. "I'm literally just an orphan who made my way to the east coast."

"She doesn't seem like a scammer anyway," Heather said. "Just the sweetest lady and her daughter, out on an adventure. Wouldn't you want her to be your sister?"

Luke's stomach tightened. Only a few nights before, he'd wanted to throw the details of his birth into the fireplace. Now, it was like the past had jumped up to bite him.

Slowly, the conversation shifted to other topics. Casey discussed her upcoming trip to Barcelona, where she planned to meet with her newest client. Grant spoke about his brother, who continued to go to AA meetings and was in the beginning stages of a divorce. Nicole spoke about the beautiful evening she'd planned at the Acadia Eatery, with no mention of any secret kissing in the back office. There was laughter and good banter, and Luke soon found himself at ease with his chosen family.

It was incredibly late and frigid, and Heather convinced him to stay the night in the main house rather than walk the mile home. Luke hadn't stayed many times at the main house. This seemed an even greater sign that he and Heather were now "really dating."

Heather sat at the antique armoire and prepared herself for the night ahead: removing her makeup and applying night serums. Luke was at the end of her bed with his legs out on either side of him and his hands clasped between. Heather reached over and smeared a bit of cream onto his cheeks, which made him laugh. He rubbed it in as Heather made a silly comment. "I know you're one year younger than me, but you still have to take care of your skin."

"You're a cougar," Luke teased her.

"Yeah. A forty-four-year-old after a forty-three-year-old."

"You know, we'll both be forty-four in a couple of weeks," Luke said.

Heather's blue eyes brightened. "What should we do for your birthday?"

Luke shrugged. "Let's just stay in bed all day."

Heather rolled her eyes and jumped onto the rickety bed beside him. She'd recently purchased a lovely mattress, top-of-the-line, but the bed beneath it seemed on its last legs. She drew a curl behind his ear and whispered, "If that's really what you want."

Luke grinned and kissed her warmly, closing his eyes. He then fell back on the mattress, bouncing slightly as Heather burrowed in beside him.

"What a day," he sighed.

"Yeah. I can't imagine what you're feeling."

"It's just weird to me that there's no death certificate. Nothing," Luke said. "I wonder how much digging she did into Glenn and Wendy."

Heather lifted her head and cocked it. "You know that I have a real history with this. Beyond searching for information within my own family, I worked as a journalist for a little while and got pretty good at searching for things online. I also still have some passcodes to databases that I probably shouldn't still have."

Luke bucked up onto his elbows. Heather hustled to grab her laptop. She then returned to the bed, crossed her legs beneath her, and began to type the names they'd only just learned that day: GLENN, WENDY, and LEO BARRINGTON.

It wasn't a simple search. If it was, Angie would have discovered their whereabouts by then. But after a thirty-five-minute search through online records, Heather piped up with bad news:

Glenn Barrington had passed away twelve years after Luke's birth.

Luke took the news strangely. It wasn't even as sad as watching someone die in a movie. It was like hearing about a friend of a friend of a friend who'd passed on. He furrowed his brow and looked at the photograph listed in the obituary, where a man in his mid-thirties (a bit younger than Luke was) stood with a thick mustache and curly hair. He looked almost exactly like Luke had maybe two or three years ago, with the added eighties flair. He'd died in Ohio.

"Wow," Luke breathed. "I don't even know what to say."

Heather gripped his wrist and kissed him gently on the cheek. "We can stop for the night if you want to."

"No. We're already in this," Luke told her. "I want to know."

Heather continued to dig. Her fingers clacked across the keyboard as she fought for more information. There were no more death certificates for Wendy or Leo. But she did find proof that one Leo Barrington had graduated from Penn State University. He was on a long list of graduates in the year 1997, the year he would have turned twenty-three. It was enough to take Luke's breath away.

"It must be him," Luke said pointedly. "The ages are right."

Heather continued on Penn State's website, hunting for some sign of Leo. After a long while, she found him in an old photograph from the 1995 chess championships. He was standing third from the left, his hands behind his back and his chest puffed out. Again, he looked remarkably like both Glenn and Luke in their early twenties. The sight of him nearly brought Luke to tears.

"No..." Luke whispered, taking the computer from Heather to gawk at the photograph.

"It's uncanny," Heather said, smacking her palms together. "Gosh. Look at the two of you!"

"What... what happened to him?" Luke's tongue threatened to choke him. "Later, I mean."

Heather continued to dig. Eventually, when nothing came up about Leo, she wrote an email to the director of the chess team at Penn State University. In 1997, the director had been only twenty-five. Now, he was nearly fifty, yet still the team director. "Maybe he knows where Leo ended up," Heather said with a shrug. "It was probably one of his first teams, and they all were around the same age. Who knows?"

When Heather searched for Wendy Barrington, nothing came up except obituaries for women without any of Wendy's features. Luke yawned and stretched his arms over his head. He suggested giving up for the night. Slowly, they fell beneath the covers and wrapped their arms around one another, burrowing themselves together. By the stroke of one at night, they fell into a deep sleep. Luke was grateful not to dream.

* * *

The following morning, Heather, Angie, Luke, and Hannah met for breakfast at the Acadia Eatery. Nicole was mad with adrenaline, cooking up eggs Benedict with fanatical zeal and mixing up near-perfect breakfast cocktails. The Acadia Eatery atmosphere was the epitome of coziness, especially with the snow falling softly outside. The conversation was bubbly, open, with Heather's enthusiasm for Angie's musical career incredibly bright.

"You saw that there's a piano over there..." Heather stated, pointing to the baby grand in the corner. "Don't you want to play for us?"

Angie blushed and glanced at her daughter.

"Mom is seriously the best pianist I've ever listened to," Hannah told them. "You have to play for us."

Angie took another sip of her mimosa, nodded, then headed for the baby grand. Hannah, who drank only water and juice, placed her hand across her stomach in a way that let Luke know she was pregnant. Luke wondered how much of this storyline fit into Angie's.

As Angie began to play a jazz standard, Heather's phone buzzed. She glanced down and then quickly opened the email, which she showed Luke was from none other than the chess team director at Penn State University.

Hello Heather.

Thanks for your email. I have a very good relationship with Leo Barrington; in fact, we frequently visit him at his home in Boston. Where was it you met him? And why are you trying to track him down?

Luke flung a hand over his mouth. In the corner, Angie fell into the beauty of the piano track, her body tilting forward and back in time. Hannah eyed them curiously but then returned her attention to her mother. Tears formed in her eyes. Throughout Luke's life, he'd always had an ear for music, despite never having had the proper training. Was this a genetic thing?

Before Angie's return to the table, Heather searched on social media for a Leo Barrington in Boston, Massachusetts. Angie's fingers crept across the keys, rousing emotion in Luke's very soul. Very soon, Heather whipped her phone around to show a social media profile for one Leo Barrington in Boston— and the third profile picture featured him and an older woman.

Beneath the photograph were the words:

"Me and Mama Wendy. The love of my life."

Chapter Twenty-Four

L ater that morning, after another in-depth Heather analysis into the goings-on of Leo Barrington's life, Luke and Angie gathered around a table with a phone on speaker and dialed Leo's number, which they had discovered on his business website. According to Heather's research, Leo owned and operated his own marketing business, based in downtown Boston. He'd recently been divorced and had two children, one girl and one boy. This was, Luke supposed, why he'd called Wendy the "love of his life." He'd been through heartache.

"Hello, this is Leo."

The voice was deep, powerful, and self-assured. Luke felt a pang of recognition alongside a pang of fear. Suppose this guy wasn't actually their brother? Suppose they were digging themselves into a pile of muck?

"Hi, Leo. My name is Luke. Do you have a minute to talk about something? It's pretty, um. Big."

"I'm not interested in buying anything," Leo told him.

"I'm not selling anything." Luke swallowed and lifted his

eyes toward Angie. "Actually, I'm sitting here with someone named Angie. Maybe she can explain why we're calling a bit better than I can."

Leo was silent but hadn't yet hung up. Over the next few minutes, Angie explained what she could about the adoption papers and the records office and what she'd learned about Wendy and Glenn Barrington. After she said their names, there was a horrible pause on the other line before Leo finally spoke.

"Wendy and Glenn are my parents," he said simply. After that, he sighed heavily and muttered something to himself, something Angie and Luke couldn't understand. After that, he cursed. Maybe this was understandable.

Finally, Leo continued. "My mother left my father a long time ago— back in Ohio. I heard that he passed away."

"He did," Luke said. "In the late eighties."

"If memory serves me right, old Glenn wasn't exactly the greatest of guys," Leo continued. "We were better off without him."

Angie had begun to cry. Luke placed a hand over hers and held it softly as Leo continued to speak.

"My mother, she saved my life," Leo continued. "We've spent most of our lives side-by-side. The past couple of years, she's taken a turn after being diagnosed with dementia. She'll probably have to spend some time in a home soon. I hate to do it, but it'll eventually be too much for me to do alone."

Luke's throat tightened. This woman, a woman who very well might have been his mother, had dementia. This meant that maybe, all memory of Angie (and maybe Luke) was lost, anyway. What did it matter?

"She has periods of clarity, though," Leo explained. "Times when I know she's sharp as a tack."

Luke and Angie made eye contact. Was this an opening?

"I just… I don't know. I don't know how much I want to rock her world with this," Leo continued.

"And I would bet that you don't know if you want to believe this," Luke told him.

"I hate to say it, but it's true."

"We'd understand it," Luke told him. "We just want to meet the two of you. Call it curiosity. Call it us trying to figure out our own dilemmas about our lives. It could just be a coffee in the afternoon. We just want to meet."

"Let me give you a call back," Leo said.

Angie and Luke sat in silence for the next fifteen minutes, both lost in their own thoughts. Luke continued to check the phone, at a loss.

"I can't believe that's my brother," Angie whispered. "I can't believe I could have grown up with an older brother."

Luke's heart banged against his ribcage. Before he could answer, Leo called him back. He lifted the phone to his ear as Leo said:

"Come out on Wednesday if you can. I live with Mom these days in the house she raised me in. I can't promise she'll be lucid. But maybe there will be enough there. I don't know. Heck, I don't know a lot of things. I just hope…" Leo trailed off, then added, "I hope you get some closure, even if she isn't your mother."

* * *

Early Wednesday morning, Luke, Angie, Heather, and Hannah clambered into Luke's truck en route to Boston, Massachusetts. Hannah insisted on taking charge of the morning's driving playlist, which put her up front with "Uncle Luke." Luke bristled at the term and then laughed outright. "Even if I'm not your Uncle Luke," he told her, "I sure do like the name."

In back, Angie and Heather swapped stories and fell into

silly giggles. Frequently, Heather said, "Angie, I can't believe what I'm hearing. I've had that same thought about a dozen times just this week!"

"I think I have a new best friend back here, Luke," Heather told him.

"Oh great," Luke offered. "I have a hunch that you two will be nothing but trouble together."

The gang arrived in Boston around two in the afternoon. Leo had sent directions to an old colonial house, painted a dark red with white shutters on either side of the small windows. Luke whistled as he parked out front.

"Is this really it?" He tried to imagine growing up in a place like this, especially when he compared it to his "real" life in foster care. The thoughts hurt.

As they got out of the truck and slammed the doors, a man in his mid-to-late-forties stepped out onto the porch and raised a hand in greeting. Luke's heart jumped into his throat. Leo stepped onto the porch staircase and lifted his chin so that Boston sunlight crept through his raucous curls.

Was this Luke's brother?

"How was the drive?" Leo asked. This was what men were supposed to ask one another, no matter how "serious" the situation was. It made everything the slightest bit more normal.

"Not bad," Luke replied as he stepped toward Leo, assessing him. They then shook hands, eyeing one another. Their faces were, in fact, very similar, along with their build. They dropped hands after an initial shake. Probably, Leo was just as freaked out as Luke was.

Angie, Heather, and Hannah jumped from the truck and greeted Leo warmly, in the way only women could. Hannah hugged him and said, "I've never been to Boston!" This opened up the conversation beautifully, with Leo saying that he had a whole list of top-tips for Boston newbies on the fridge.

"I moved here when I was four years old, so I don't really

know any other life," Leo said as they stepped into the foyer of the old-world house. "Mom still has her Ohio accent, but me? I feel more Boston than anything else."

Luke and Angie exchanged glances. This was terribly eerie.

After Leo closed the door behind them, Heather slipped a hand through Luke's and gave him a firm glance that said, "I'm here for you." He nodded back.

"Mom just got up from her nap," Leo said tentatively. "She's in the living room. I told her about you, but I'm not sure if she fully understood what I meant. Maybe that means that it didn't happen at all? Or maybe it means that she just doesn't remember? It's hard to say."

Luke's throat tightened. They followed after Leo into the main living room, where a woman in her late sixties sat in the corner on an overstuffed armchair, gazing into the flickering fire.

"Mom? Remember those people I told you about?" Leo said as they entered the room. "They've come all the way from Bar Harbor."

For a long moment, Wendy Barrington's crumpled face gave no recognition. Luke sat across from her on a mustard-colored sofa and wished that they'd never come all this way. Hadn't he been happier before Angie had darkened his door?

Actually, he wasn't sure about that, either.

"Wendy. Wendy Barrington?" Luke asked her.

At this, the older woman scrunched her nose angrily. "No, not Barrington. Not any longer," she told him. "That evil man. Glenn. I can't believe I ever married him."

Leo remained standing between Luke, Angie, Hannah, Heather, and his mother, Wendy. He looked ready to jump between them and protect his mother at any moment.

"I only did because I got pregnant," Wendy added, lifting her finger into the air.

At this, Hannah leaned toward Angie and whispered, "See? I'm doing the right thing." Luke hardly heard it, but it was there.

"You look just like him," Wendy told Luke then, her eyebrows lowering. "Just like him indeed."

Luke's stomach curdled at the thought. He dropped his eyes toward the ground, both disgusted and fearful. Was he ruining this older woman's mental state by being there?

Luke tried to think of what to say next. Anything.

But through his struggles, he forgot to reckon for Angie, who was much stronger than he was.

"Wendy?" Angie piped up, her eyes glistening. "Wendy, I — I hate to ask you this. But I've come all this way from the Midwest and I have to ask. Do you remember your daughter Angela at all?"

It was like dropping a bomb. Leo turned himself violently toward Angie, his eyes wide, and said, "She's really not fit for this."

But in the same moment, Wendy's mouth formed a wide O as she took in the full meaning of Angie's words.

"Nobody has said that to me— that name. Not in forty-five years," she whispered.

Angie blinked quickly so that tears flickered from her eyes.

Wendy's lips quivered with shock. She took a tissue from the nearby box and dotted it near her eyes.

"I just kept getting pregnant," Wendy said, sounding suddenly so helpless. "One morning, I awoke and had three children that I couldn't fully care for. There was Leo, who took the brunt of Glenn's blows. And then there was Angela and the newborn baby. Luke." Wendy's eyes continued to widen, as though she hardly believed her story.

Leo muttered under his breath, "I've never heard this before in my life."

"He was having another go at Leo," Wendy said softly.

"Punching him against the side of the head. Leo was only four years old— *four*. And I knew that the other two were next. When the new baby cried, I feared for his life. If Glenn didn't kill him then, he would certainly try to kill him later."

Luke's heart shattered at the image. Had his first ten days really been marred with such violence?

"The baby wasn't old." Wendy whacked her hands to her forehead and gaped at the window. "Not old at all. But he wouldn't stop crying and Angela joined in. She was so loud. So terribly loud. And Glenn threatened to kill us all in our beds. I just... I hardly remember..."

Wendy lifted her hands in the air and studied her fingers contemplatively. "I had to get them out. I drove the three of them to the orphanage. I couldn't care for them. I had no skills. No money. Nothing. I just had to free them from the world I'd created for them. I had to..." She shook her head tentatively.

"Oh my god." Leo breathed.

Suddenly, Wendy's eyes alight, she lifted her chin to match Leo's gaze. It was as though the previous Wendy had been at a distance, while this current Wendy was very much with them. She knew who was there. She knew who she affected.

"You ran after me," Wendy whispered. "You screamed at me not to leave you there. Angie and Luke were too young. Too confused. But you. You looked at me, and you demanded that I..."

Wendy burst into a round of coughing. Nobody knew what to do. Finally, Hannah hustled for the kitchen and reappeared with a glass of water, which Wendy accepted gratefully.

"My sister had a room on the east coast," Wendy continued, her voice raspy and low. "And Leo and I drove all the way here to Boston to start a new life away from Glenn and Ohio. And every single day since then, I've ached, knowing that I left my babies behind. I always hoped that despite my horrible actions, they still had a good life. Somehow."

* * *

Wendy returned to her bedroom for another nap no more than ten minutes later. Luke pressed his fingers into his eyes until he saw bright spots. When he lifted his head, he witnessed Angie and Leo in a similar state of shock.

"That was quite a story," Leo whispered.

"Do you remember any of it?" Angie asked suddenly, almost pleading.

Leo shook his head. "I don't know. It's all so cloudy. And Mom never talked about it. All those years, I thought I was the only child she'd ever had."

Leo pressed his hands on his thighs and said, "Let me go look at the old paperwork in the computer room. Maybe there's something there." He jumped up and headed off, his joints creaking as he went. Two minutes later, he reappeared with a crate of old documents, which he explained his mother had brought from Ohio when they'd initially "escaped."

"I remember Glenn a little bit," he explained as he leafed through the paperwork and the photographs. "When she says he beat me, I remember the blows. Flashing images and all the fear. I've been in therapy since my twenties because of it."

"I'm so sorry," Angie breathed, her nostrils flaring.

"You can see how much he broke Mom," Leo continued. "I've always wondered what kind of woman she was before she met Dad. I see it sometimes. How alive she must have been. How playful. She was a brilliant grandmother to my kids. She was always coming up with a new game to play. Always ready with a joke. But the darkness got to her. She resisted therapy. It's just not something her generation did. But she really could have benefited from it."

He then paused to add: "I can't imagine what you must be feeling." He pressed his hand across his forehead and whispered, "I can't believe she planned to give us all up."

Luke so wanted to tell him that he'd "made the cut," but he resisted. It didn't matter. The cards had fallen. There was no going back.

After a full fifteen minutes of quiet searching, Leo drew up something that made Luke's head spin.

It was a birth certificate for one Luke Barrington.

February 16, 1978.

Seven pounds, nine ounces.

Luke clutched the birth certificate with shaking hands. This was, after all, what he'd wanted from Angie to "prove" his past. Did he feel that this was his reality now? He wasn't sure.

But it did seem like proof.

Angie looked at the old certificate and then placed her hand on Luke's shoulder. Upstairs, their mother slept through a nap, fitful from dementia, yet able to remember one fateful night when she'd given them up.

"Where should we go from here?" Angie asked him, her eyes widening.

"I have no idea," Luke said. "But I guess we should do it together. What do you think?"

Chapter Twenty-Five

The apartment on Firefly Lane in downtown Bar Harbor offered a six-month lease. *Six months*, Angie and Hannah told one another. That's all they needed to figure out what came next. "Whatever it is," Hannah liked to say, "I'll be ready for it."

The apartment was just three rooms: a combined living room and kitchen, plus two bedrooms. The bathroom had a stand-up shower and a sink that often spit out water rather than streamed it. The rent was far cheaper than anything Angie had ever read about in downtown Chicago.

On the drive back from their meeting with Leo and Wendy, Angie and Hannah had sat in the backseat of Luke's truck and texted back and forth about what to do next. They'd driven across the country. They'd met Angie's birth mother and two brothers. Had it changed anything? Of course. But what did that mean for their lives?

HANNAH: I think we should stick by Luke and Heather. They're beautiful people. And I like the

idea of staying away from Chicago for a while. Running away. You with me, Louise?

ANGIE: Always, Thelma.

It was February 16th, which meant that Luke, Uncle Luke, Luke the younger brother, was turning forty-four. Heather had planned a beautiful birthday party at the Keating Inn, and both Angie and Hannah had been invited. Now, hours before the celebration, mother and daughter squabbled about what to wear. It would be their real "introduction" to the people of Bar Harbor, a place they'd decided would be their home. It was a big deal. Hannah, pregnant, thought every dress made her look "fat." Angie didn't know how to argue with her. Ultimately, her excitement for her grandbaby and this newfound life on the coast filled her with overzealous joy. Why did Hannah care about some party dress? Their world was different now. It belonged to them and no one else.

"Where are your gold bands?" Hannah ducked out of the bathroom, her eyes wide as she hunted for Angie's earrings, which they'd purchased together at a boutique several afternoons before.

"On the nightstand," Angie told her. "In my bedroom."

Hannah disappeared and then came back out to the living room with glorious dancing earrings, which highlighted her dark eyes. Angie's heart jumped with gladness.

"Do you really think Leo will show up?" Hannah asked as she sat at the edge of the couch. She placed her fist at the base of her chin and watched her mother contemplatively. Every day seemed a new adventure.

"I have no idea," Angie returned. "We haven't heard from him very much since the Boston trip."

"It's probably a lot to take in," Hannah said. "The fact that you had these other siblings who didn't grow up with you..."

Angie's stomach tightened. In truth, the story had hit her like a ton of bricks. Her elder brother had been allowed the nourishing presence of their mother, while she and Luke had been cast out to other storylines. One night, she'd spent nearly six hours curled around the toilet, puking when necessary. Why not her? Why not Luke? Why just Leo? What had gone on in that woman's head all the way back in 1978?

At six o'clock, Angie and Hannah arrived at the Keating Inn and Acadia Eatery for Luke's forty-forth birthday. Nicole had baked an elaborate and gorgeous birthday cake with beautiful flower detail, plus the words, "YOU ARE OLD." Luke groaned yet laughed wildly when he saw it beneath twelve flickering candles.

"You're a monster," he told Nicole. "Thank you."

As the thirty-plus number of guests sang him a happy birthday, Luke placed one arm around Heather's waist and one over Angie's shoulder. Over the previous two weeks, the two had gotten closer than ever, swapping stories from their life and finding common ground. Angie found that their sense of humor was linked tremendously and joked that this was a genetic thing. Hannah had continued to call him "Uncle Luke," and he hadn't protested once.

They'd begun a new life.

A couple of hours into Luke's birthday festivities, Angie spotted them at the doorway.

Leo and Wendy Barrington.

Wendy wore a dark purple dress, and her grey hair had been styled so that it curled around her ears. She blinked around the Acadia Eatery with nervous yet excited eyes while her eldest son, Leo, gripped her arm lovingly. He looked just as anxious as she did. When his eyes found Angie's, he nearly leaped from his skin.

Angie, Luke, and Leo analyzed one another for a long moment. The music continued to blare from the loudspeaker as the rest of the Bar Harbor crew carried on the party. Angie wasn't sure how they could go on from there. Perhaps she and

Luke were too awkward to make any sort of amends with their mother and other brother. Maybe it was too late.

But suddenly, Wendy Barrington bucked away from Leo and shot straight for the baby grand piano in the corner. With a flourish, she sat at the piano and extended her beautiful fingers over the keys. Angie's heart nearly shattered in her chest. She whipped around to tell someone to turn down the music. It happened just as Wendy began to play a beautiful tune from another era.

The song was called "Dream of Love," and it was written approximately three hundred years ago all the way in Europe. Angie knew it well, as she'd practiced it for three months straight when she'd been seventeen. She couldn't believe her mother knew it so well.

"Wow..." Luke said under his breath, eyeing the mother who'd given them life. "She is very talented."

Angie could have fallen to her knees. But instead, she walked like a ghost to her mother at the piano and leaned against the vibrating baby grand, watching her mother's face. Her mother, who'd forgotten so much due to dementia, remembered this song by heart. There was no telling where their relationship would go from there. But in Angie's mind and heart, music was a perfect way to start anything. She closed her eyes and allowed herself to dream.

Coming Next in the Bar Harbor Series

Pre order Glistening Sunsets

Other Books by Katie

The Vineyard Sunset Series

Secrets of Mackinac Island Series

Sisters of Edgartown Series

A Katama Bay Series

A Mount Desert Island Series

Connect with Katie Winters

BookBub
Amazon
Facebook
Newsletter
To receive exclusive updates from Katie Winters please sign up
to be on her Newsletter!
CLICK HERE TO SUBSCRIBE